i

# AfterLife

## The Adventures of a Lost Soul

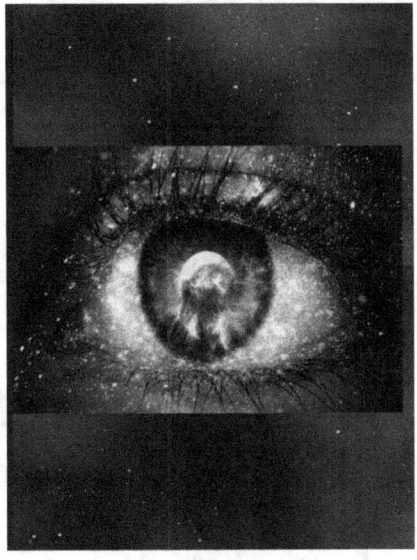

by

## Matthew J. Pallamary

*Mystic Ink Publishing*

*Mystic Ink Publishing*
*San Diego, CA*
*www.mysticinkpublishing.com*

*ISBN 10: 0-9986809-3-1 (sc)*
*ISBN 13: 978-0-9986809-3-4 (sc)*
*Printed in the United States of America*
*San Bernardino, California*

*This book is printed on acid-free papermade from 30% post-consumer waste recycled material.*

*Library of Congress Control Number: 2018911226*
*Book Jacket and Page Design: Matthew J. Pallamary/San DiegoCA*
*Author's Photograph: Matthew J. Pallamary -- Gibbs Photo/Malibu CA*

# DEDICATION

This book is dedicated to Colleen Kennedy aka M.A.

"There exists certain wandering unclean spirits who have lost their heavenly activities from being weighed down by earthly passions and disorders. So then these spirits, burdened with sin and steeped in vice, who have sacrificed their original simplicity, being themselves lost, unceasingly strive to destroy others, as a consolation for their own misfortune; depraved themselves, they strive to communicate error and depravity to others; estranged from God, they strive to alienate others by the introduction of vicious forms of religion. Poets know these spirits as "demons"....
For they both deceive and are deceived; being ignorant of pure truth, to their own destruction they are afraid to confess that which they do know. Thus they weigh down men's minds and draw them from heaven, call them away from the true God to material things, disturb their lives and trouble their sleep; stealthily creeping into men's bodies, thanks to their rarefied and subtle nature, they counterfeit diseases, terrify the imagination, rack the limbs, to compel men to worship them; then, sated with the fumes from the altars and the slaughter of beasts, they undo what they have tied themselves, so as to appear to have effected a cure. They are also responsible for madmen, whom you see running out into the streets, themselves soothsayers of a kind but without a temple, raging, ranting, whirling round in the dance; there is the same demoniacal possession, but the object of the frenzy is different.

Marcus Minucius Felix

Darkness.

Numb and disoriented, Steve opened his eyes.

Several people crowded around a van. He craned his neck to see what was going on but they blocked his view. He reached out to tap someone on the shoulder and jerked his hand back, shocked when his finger went *through* them.

He examined his hand and gasped when he saw through it, then he looked down. His body had the same translucent quality. Without thinking he walked through the bodies of the people in the crowd as if *they* were ethereal, stopping dead when he made it to the front of the crowd.

A motorcycle identical to his Harley lay crushed beneath the van, a mangled body twisted within the wreckage. He stumbled around to the other side of the wreck and stared at it. One glazed eye glared back at him and the other dangled halfway down its cheek. His knees gave way and he sagged as darkness claimed him once again. He struggled to rationalize it all as a dream, but its surrealistic quality heightened its vividness, and with this hyper-lucidity the answer became clear.

*I'm dead!*

The sight of his blood-soaked mutilated body stunned him, but the full blow hit when he turned and saw the ashen faces of Jon, Jaret, and Amanda frozen in horrified grimaces. He ran to them screaming, but no one acknowledged him. Amanda buried her head in Jaret's shoulder and sobbed, while Jaret and Jon looked on, helpless. Overcome with emotion, Steve tried to speak again, but all that came out were unintelligible sounds and his despair turned from anger to frustration, followed by hopelessness. He couldn't remember ever feeling such anguish.

As if mocking his suffering, his emotional turmoil had no physical sensations. He cried without tears, feared without chills or dryness of throat and felt nothing on his skin except a muted sense of touch as if a giant glove encased his whole body. The textures and temperatures of normal sensations had gone.

He felt the pull of gravity holding him down, but he had no sense of weight and his perceptions went no further than his emotions. As his initial shock faded the full weight of what happened enveloped him like an unwelcome fog rolling in off the ocean bringing with it a gauzy sense of separation from the people he loved, particularly Heather. His longing for her filled him with an acute sense of loss as though some vital part of his anatomy had been torn out.

An ambulance came and he stared in silence as paramedics extricated his battered body from the wreckage and put a sheet over it.

# LIFE

# CHAPTER ONE

Steve Hanson awoke in the middle of his living room floor to a blinding white light. "What the fu..." His heart raced. He blinked, making his head throb with alternating sharp and dull pulses. He closed his eyes to escape the bright pain coming through his apartment window and rolled his head away from the light, opening them to see a half empty fifth of Jack Daniels. His heart constricted when he saw a gold pentagram pendant with strange symbols inscribed on it beside the bottle.

Shit, blacked out again, he thought with a sinking feeling. I'm never going to put my life back together if I keep this shit up.

He closed his eyes and remained still for a long time breathing deep to calm his fluttering heart before forcing himself to sit up. The movement made his head pound harder. Stepping over his treasured Taylor acoustic guitar, he groped his way to the bathroom and downed two Excedrin before studying the puffy face staring back at him from the mirror. His angular features and close-trimmed beard contrasted two bloodshot brown eyes peering out from under his spiky short black hair.

"You are one ugly ass motherfucker," he said to the mirror. "Did your mother have any kids that lived?"

He shuffled into the kitchen and downed a glass of cold water, soothing his parched throat, then he popped a Dunkin' Donuts K-cup into his Keurig and lit a Marlboro, struggling to remember the previous night's events.

Oddly enough the night started on a positive note with his first karate class where he sparred with a brown belt named Mick. At first it didn't seem like a fair match. A couple of years younger and a little smaller than Steve, Mick looked like a California surfer with blond hair and blue eyes. Steve didn't know what to make of him, but liked him because of the way Mick looked him in the eye when he spoke with a direct committed look that held no malice.

"How are you doing?" Mick extended his gloved hand. "My name's Mick."

Steve nodded, meeting Mick's glove with a tap. "Pleased to meet you. I'm Steve." I'm going to have fun with this one, he thought, believing he could intimidate Mick with his bigger one-hundred-eighty pound frame and longer reach. He lunged at Mick trying to catch him off guard.

Mick sidestepped and caught him in the stomach with a well placed foot that winded him and he realized that Mick could have kicked him a lot harder. He wheeled around to face Mick again and saw a lopsided smile.

Steve tried again and again but couldn't land a solid punch. The glancing ones he did land, he sensed that Mick gave him. Mick didn't hit hard with his counter punches, but every one of them found its mark. He also kicked up toward Steve's face, stopping his foot inches from Steve's nose before tapping him with it which infuriated Steve, causing him to swing wild, but he kept missing. Mick danced and sidestepped, his cock-eyed smile showing how much he was enjoying himself.

Soon, Steve staggered back gasping, thinking, little bastard's playing with me!

Following that thought, Mick went to work picking Steve apart, his punches and kicks landing hard enough to let Steve know who was in control without going overboard. They bowed to each other and tapped gloves when the match was over. Steve thought he should be mad about being beaten, but Mick had humbled him in a friendly manner without the least bit of arrogance.

"Hey buddy," Mick said when class was over, "You didn't do too bad." He patted Steve on the back. "You just have to relax a little more."

Steve shook his head. "Are you kidding? You spanked me good for a little Cali surfer boy!"

"I've just been coming longer," Mick said waving his finger, "and I ain't no little Cali surfer boy. I grew up in Boston."

"No shit? What part?"

"Dorchester," Mick said, heavy on the first syllable with an accent that Steve heard as Dawchestah.

"I'm from Newton."

"I won't hold that against you." Mick's lopsided smile returned, combined with a wink.

"Listen," Steve said staring at the floor. "Sorry about losing my temper. I was out of line. I let my ego get in the way."

"Don't worry about it," Mick said with a dismissive wave. "I did the same thing when I first came here."

"My apartment is only a block away," Steve said, surprising himself. "You want to stop by for a nightcap on the way home? I'm new here and don't really know anybody."

Mick stuck out his hand and they shook. "You do now."

They left the studio and walked to Steve's Ocean Beach apartment where he poured himself a shot of whiskey. When he went to pour a second one Mick held up his hand.

"Just water for me, thanks."

Steve downed his shot and got Mick a bottled water from the fridge.

"What made you decide to move here to O.B.?" Mick said.

"I needed a change of scene." Steve handed him the water. "I got a great job offer, so I sold everything I had, hopped on a plane and here I am. It was one of the smartest things I ever did. What about you?"

Mick sipped his water. "Been here for about six years now. I got pretty deep into the drug scene back in Dot., but when the bullets started flying and my buddies started dying and doing hard time I moved out here and left all that behind."

"Why San Diego?"

"It was the furthest I could get from Dorchester without leaving the country." He held up his bottle. "Now you could say I'm on a natural high." His clear blue eyes blazed as he spoke and the conviction in his voice said that he spoke his truth. Mick pointed at Steve's Taylor standing up in the corner. "You play?"

Steve downed a second shot, grabbed the bottle of Jack Daniels and sat down on the floor with the guitar and bottle and started playing.

He had no memory of the rest of the night and the harder he tried to recall it, the vaguer things became, so he snuffed out his cigarette, drank his coffee and hit the shower. Twenty minutes later he almost felt human again. He picked up the previous night's remains in the living room and tossed the gold pendant into a junk drawer. Out of sight, out of mind.

Anxious to put his morning's painful awakening out of his mind he grabbed his motorcycle helmet and briefcase. No one would be in the office today so he could catch up on the source code he needed to make the deadline he promised. He put on his jacket and headed out into another San Diego day. The blue sky, scattered clouds, and light ocean breeze never failed to invigorate him. After spending the winter in Boston, living in Ocean Beach wasn't hard to take.

He strapped his briefcase to his Harley's luggage rack, put on his helmet, and rode a few blocks to the stop light marking the entrance to I-8. When the light turned green he opened the throttle full bore onto the freeway. The acceleration gave him a thrill as he shifted up through the gears, weaving his way through the morning traffic enjoying the wind on his face and the feeling of his Harley beneath him responding to his every whim.

He approached the interchange that took him North on 163 and slowed, then felt an urge to open the throttle.

The engine responded taking him straight for the guardrail.

# CHAPTER TWO

He hit the brakes and downshifted at the last moment. His rear tire broke loose and he skidded sideways, missing the guardrail by inches.

"You stupid ass!"

He hit the gas and accelerated out of the turn and took deep breaths to calm himself and stop the shaking. What possessed me to do that crazy shit? I've had those urges before, and yeah, sometimes I push the limits, but nothing like aiming for the guardrail. When I played chicken with myself before I had control, but now it feels like it's controlling me, especially since Carla...

Since meeting her his life had become a drunken blur. He couldn't remember half of what he did and his compulsive urges and blackouts came more and more. Now they intruded into his life without drinking. His thoughts felt different too. Like they belonged to someone else. At first he ignored them, but as time passed they came stronger. Some times he had the impulse to drive off the road or slam into somebody like just now. Other times he felt compelled to fly down the street as fast as he could like something else controlled him. He had no idea where his self-destructive urges came from, but they started after Carla...

His band Triple Threat had a gig playing a private party at an old mansion near Hyannis on Cape Cod. Steve played lead and shared vocals with Butch, a lanky, tatted, long brown haired, bearded virtuoso who rocked it with solid bass lines. Their drummer, short stocky Muscle Man Charlie sang backup and pushed the music relentlessly forward with a solid driving beat, accented by maniacal blue eyes that blazed beneath a mop of shaggy blond hair.

Butch, Charlie, and Steve all felt uncomfortable with the peculiar group of goths they played for. They all wore black and had silver jewelry, piercings and cryptic tattoos. A lot of them had a thing for pentagrams, but as bizarre as the whole scene was, they were being paid an unusually large sum for the gig, so they ignored their discomfort and concentrated on having a good time with the music.

In the middle of a wailing guitar solo while playing The Rolling Stones *Sympathy for the Devil,* Steve looked up, instantly mesmerized by dark seductive eyes that held him spellbound. She had the body and movements of a dancer, a mane of long black hair, and full sensuous lips. They studied each other for a long time and Steve felt something pass between them that he could only describe as telepathic, then she smiled and turned, shaking the most perfect ass he had ever seen.

When the gig ended and they started breaking down their gear, he couldn't stop looking in her direction. Each time their eyes met he felt a silent communication. Like the proverbial moth to a flame he stopped what he was doing and went over to where she sat and pulled a chair up beside her.

"Hi – I – uh – er – damn!" Fucking mush mouth, he thought. Can't even think straight. "I'm sure you've heard this line a thousand times before..." He looked down at the floor then looked up and fell into the inviting gaze of her wide brown eyes. Her low cut blouse showed prominent breasts accented by a gold pentagram pendant nestled in her cleavage. Exotic looking rings bearing strange symbols glittered on long slender fingers and her perfume intoxicated him.

"My name's Carla." Her throaty voice caressed him with soft, velvety sensuality. "I really like the way you play."

"Thank you." He flushed." My name's Steve. "Listen," he heard himself saying as if someone else spoke for him. "Do you want to join me for a late night breakfast at Denny's?"

Steve shook his head at the memory and hit the gas, accelerating across northbound Saturday morning traffic until he hit the fast lane moving a little too fast, the same way his life with Carla had. Looking back, all he had known was passionate bliss. He couldn't understand why Butch and Charlie couldn't see it the way he did. Now after all that happened he had to admit that the signs were there from the start.

Charlie was the first to mention it, proving the old cliché that love is blind, but was it really love, or infatuation?

"What do you mean she's moving in with you?" Charlie said, spinning a drumstick between his fingers while they waited for Butch to come to rehearsal. "You've only been going together for a couple of weeks."

"I can't explain it," Steve said, his mind still caught up in his intimate time with Carla from the night before, "but I'm crazy about her and she needs me."

"Needs you? Don't you think you're rushing things?"

"Listen, man, all I can say is I care for her." Steve started pacing. "Something happened to her in her past. I don't know what and she doesn't want to talk about it, but it must have been pretty bad. I'm going to make sure nothing ever happens to her again."

Charlie switched hands and resumed his spinning. "Just make sure you don't get yourself screwed over riding in on your white horse to save the day. You look like hell. You feeling all right?"

"Yeah." Steve rubbed his temples. "I'm OK. I haven't been sleeping too good so I'm a little under the weather, but it'll pass."

Charlie frowned. "She has you that uptight?"

Steve waved his hand. "It's not her, It's me. I've been having these weird dreams lately..."

"Maybe you'd better slow down a little. What's the big rush? Maybe you're thinking too much with the wrong head." Charlie smiled mischievously and grabbed his crotch. "Know what I mean?"

Steve tensed at the thought and glanced down at his speedometer which was hitting ninety. Shit. I should've listened to Charlie. He eased off the throttle. Back then he didn't listen to anybody else either. His infatuation with Carla had blocked out any signs of weirdness. He should have paid attention to the weird shit when he moved her into his apartment.

What the hell's in this box, he thought when he pulled it out of the back of a truck that Carla's quirky friends had helped load. Fucking thing weighs a ton. He tried hefting it to his shoulder and turned toward the apartment building when his shirt caught on the tail gate. He lost his balance and the box slipped to the ground, splitting one of its corners. A tiny skull rolled out.

"What the?" He picked it up and examined it, then opened the box and peered inside to see more animal skulls, a large ceremonial dagger, and a gold chalice, all of them bearing black pentagrams. Feeling oddly exposed like he was doing something wrong, he looked around to see if anyone was watching, then stuffed everything back in the box and hurried up the steps to his apartment.

"Hey, Carla, sorry, but I fell with this box and it broke open. What *is* this shit?"

She froze and her face drained of color. "It's nothing," she said a little too quickly. "Just some stuff left over from an anthropology project."

"You OK?"

"I'm fine." She turned her back. "I'm a little tired from all this moving, that's all. Stick that box in the closet. I'll deal with it later."

"I didn't know you studied anthropology. You must have studied some pretty bizarre cultures."

She let out a high pitched giggle. "Yeah, pretty bizarre, that's for sure."

He checked his speedometer and saw that his speed had crept up again, so he slowed. That incident made him a little uneasy, but his ongoing infatuation with Carla and her insatiable passion, not to mention the amazing sex they had after she moved in kept him blinded, and once more he ignored the signs from his closest friends, like when he held up his hand and showed off his wedding band when he walked into a rehearsal.

"You gotta be shitting me!" Butch said.

"You can't be serious," Charlie added.

"Why not?"

"You've only been with her for a month," Charlie said as he hung up a cymbal. "Please, tell me this is a joke."

"Hey, fuck you guys! I take a big step in my life and all you do is piss and moan."

Charlie looked solemnly at Butch. "He's serious."

Butch shrugged and held his hands out. "Delirious if you ask me."

"You bet your ass I'm serious!"

Butch Stood. "Calm down, brother. This isn't like you. Chill out dude. You don't look so good." He put a hand on Steve's shoulder.

"What the fuck you talking about? I don't look so good! Shit!" Steve pushed Butch's hand off his shoulder.

Butch scowled and Charlie got between them.

"Hey we're brothers, remember? All Butch is saying is that you look worn out. You been sick? Partying too much?" He arched his eyebrows. "Too much of the wild thing?"

Steve glared at Charlie. "Leave me the fuck alone, all right? It's none of your God-damned business what I've been doing." He pushed Charlie aside and stormed out the door.

That night Steve fell into a deep sleep and things got even weirder in a semi-lucid dream that felt more real than being awake.

He remembered looking up from an altar. Nude. Thirteen murmuring figures in black hooded robes surrounded him, each holding a dagger like the one from the box. They passed a gold chalice between them and each took a sip. Rivulets of red ran down the corners of their mouth when they drank.

The murmurings sounded familiar, but he couldn't understand them, then he recognized one voice. Carla's. He wanted to scream but something held his eyes closed. When the vision faded he still heard Carla's voice chanting, then he forced open his eyes and saw her leaning over him.

He sat up in bed and rubbed his eyes. "What are you doing?"

"Checking on you, honey." She kissed his forehead. "You OK?"

He nodded. "Yeah, I was having a weird dream."

"I know." She kissed him again. "Go back to sleep, honey."

That memory sent a chill through him that shook him to his core, jolting him back to the present. Looking up, he realized he was about to miss his exit, so he glanced back and leaned into his bike, cutting across several lanes of traffic, just making the exit. That maneuver following his disturbing memory left him shaking again, but very much awake and aware. He took a deep breath and let it out slowly while braking for the stop sign at the end of the exit ramp. "Jesus," he muttered, "pay attention fool or you *will* be a sacrifice." He kept breathing deep in and out getting his composure back while taking his time, deliberately navigating the last few blocks to work at slow speed.

The end came in smaller increments, but the final blows hit like a one-two-three combination punch. The first shot came at what should have been an awesome gig at Rabbit's Habit, a popular Boston nightclub that boasted a huge dance floor. Between sets, Carla sat with her friends at one table and Steve sat with the band at another. Even then he didn't feel comfortable around them and Charlie and Butch refused to have anything to do with them. It wasn't anything overt, but he always felt like an outsider whenever he was around them.

As if reading his thoughts, Charlie eyed them from across the room, asking, "Does she always have to bring those fucking weirdos?"

Steve slammed his drink down. "What's wrong with them?"

"I'll tell you what's wrong with them, they're fucking spooky. Haven't you noticed? Every time they show up the rest of the people in the club clear out."

"I wouldn't want to go through airport security with those motherfuckers," Butch said. "With all the piercings and bling and shit they have we'd never make it onto the plane on time."

Charlie giggled at that. "Seriously though, the way some of them look at me, dudes and chicks – like they're hungry and want to eat me or something. They give me the fucking heebie-jeebies. And they have those weird ass tats to boot!"

"Fucking vampires," Butch added.

"That could be," Charlie said. "I do think they suck."

Steve downed the last of his drink. "All right, enough of that shit!"

No one spoke for a minute. Butch looked thoughtful, then, "I do know one thing, everything has turned to shit since you started bringing them around."

"What do you mean?"

"Look at us right now. We never argued like this before and it seems like that's all we've been doing lately. Before Carla came along it was all about the music. Everything else was secondary to it and we weren't having all these petty bullshit arguments."

Charlie nodded, backing up what Butch said.

Steve felt like they were ganging up on him. "Bullshit!" He stood and turned away from the table. "You guys blame everything on her."

"What's happening to you, man?" Charlie said, lowering his voice. "You're not the same Steve I've known all these years. Carla's got you by the short and curlies and she has you wound up so tight you're pussy whipped and you're going to pop."

Steve glared back at them and stormed up to the stage. Butch and Charlie followed in silence and they didn't talk for the rest of the night. When the gig was over, Butch and Charlie went off together. Feeling uneasy, Steve joined Carla and her friends for a few minutes which seemed to make things worse. He didn't belong with them. He needed to apologize and set things straight with Butch and Charlie, so he went off to find them and heard their muffled voices coming from behind the door of the men's room.

"We've got to do something about Steve's old lady," Butch said, "She's really doing a number on his head."

"I know," Charlie answered, "Since she and her oddball goth freak show posse started hanging around nothing's gone right, and all we do is bicker."

"Steve's been acting like two different people."

"Like he's possessed. A regular Jekyll and Hyde. I've never seen this ugly side of him before."

"Pussy possessed."

They both chuckled.

"He acts paranoid whenever we're around," Butch continued. "I hate feeling like he doesn't trust us."

"He's got no reason."

"I know what you mean. He says one thing, then does the opposite. If you ask him about it later he says he doesn't remember. I'm telling you Charlie, he's not the same since he met her."

"She's a snake."

"And Steve's been bit."

"Somebody's going to have to talk to him."

"Who's it going to be?"

"Let's flip a coin."

They're jealous of me and Carla, Steve thought as he hurried away from the men's room before they came out. We'll see about this little talk.

He woke up the next morning to the ringing of the phone, feeling like he was talking from the bottom of a deep well. "Hullo?"

"Steve?"

"Yeah."

"It's Charlie."

"What's up?"

"Listen, I hate to be the one to tell you this, but I got stuck with it."

"What?"

"Butch and I had a meeting to talk about our problems?"

"Why didn't you guys call me?"

"Because you're part of the problem."

"What do you mean?"

"Well, it's not really you. It's Carla."

"Carla?"

"You don't see what she's like when you're not around. I know you think you love her, but you've got to cut her loose from the band man. She's trouble."

"What do you mean trouble?"

"She makes us all miserable. She did from the start."

"I find that hard to believe."

"Be reasonable man. She's affected you in a bad way. You haven't been yourself."

"How come everybody knows about this except me?"

"We didn't want you to get hurt Bro, but things have gotten out of hand."

"You guys piss me off. Holding secret meetings behind my back. I heard you talking about me last night. I'll tell you what's the matter. You're jealous!"

"Something's wrong with that broad, Steve. She's spooky. She gave me the heebie-jeebies the first time I met her at that weird ass party in Hyannis. Not only is she spooky, but that cult freak show crowd she runs with is even weirder. Butch and I think they're a bunch of devil worshipers or something."

"Get the fuck out of here! You're nuts Charlie. You guys are fucking paranoid. If you can't accept her, you can take the band and shove it!"

"But Steve..."

The line went dead.

Steve stared at his cell phone in dismay.

That night he ended up staring at himself in the mirror behind a bar. His eyes looked dark, sunken and bloodshot, and his hair looked matted and disheveled. He took another shot of whiskey.

"Charlie's right," he mumbled. "You do look like shit – and you haven't been yourself."

He heard Charlie's voice in his mind. "Carla's got you by the short and curlies."

He rapped on the bar with his knuckles. "Another!"

He drained the glass and pushed away from the bar, losing his balance in the process and falling over backward, taking a stool with him. When he tried to hoist himself up over the rim of the bar his fingers slipped and darkness took him.

When he next opened his eyes, he was staring down at the gray waters below from the Mystic River bridge.

"Jump!" a voice said, startling him. He lost his balance and teetered on the edge for an infinite moment before gathering all his energy to throw himself backward onto the narrow walkway. After falling and rolling he looked up at the steel pipe railing in disbelief, then up and down the vacant walkway.

Not a soul.

He had no other memories of that night, but that incident became a turning point that sent him in an entirely different direction at an accelerated pace. After his disappointing split with the band, Carla encouraged him to finish the last couple of classes he needed to get his degree and get a "real job". Soon after that they moved out of their crowded apartment into a rented house in Quincy and Steve started looking for serious work in earnest.

On a brisk, moonlit October night he returned from a promising job interview in San Diego. He had planned to be gone for a few days, but things went better than anticipated and he was offered a job, so he came home early to celebrate. After a delayed flight he made it home at midnight. Instead of calling he decided to surprise Carla with some roses.

Puzzled by all the cars lining the street in front of his house, he felt even more confused when he saw the flicker of candlelight through the drawn curtains. Was she expecting him? How...

He walked up the path and peered into the living room window beneath a pulled shade and saw a low altar set up in the living room. Above it hung a large gold ornament in the shape of a pentagram with an inverted crucifix in its center.

Carla's "friends" were all naked and paired off in male-female pairs, each man lying between the legs of a woman. The low murmur of their chants droned, "Say-tan. Say-tan."

Steve looked for Carla in a panic and couldn't see her. When he did it felt like a massive fist slammed him in the gut.

She lay nude on the altar. A young dark-skinned man wearing nothing but a hooded black stole prepared to mount her as another man read from a battered leather-bound book.

"*In nomine Patris et Filii et Spiritus Sancti et domini nostri Satanas.*"

Steve felt something snap inside of him and he slammed open the front door. "What the hell is going on?"

Everyone froze.

"Steve!" Tears welled up in Carla's eyes and her voice trailed off into sobs.

He crossed the room and the man with the book stepped in front of him. A right hook sent him sprawling to the floor, then Steve ripped down the tapestry and covered Carla with it.

"Come, my brother," the young man in the black stole said calmly. "Join us. There's no need to be upset."

"What?"

"St-Steve, please..." Carla pleaded.

"What do you take me for, some half-witted asshole?"

"P-Please Steve," she whispered. "Let me explain."

"There's nothing to explain." He pulled down the pentagram. "This shit isn't staying in my house another minute. Out!" He bellowed, flinging it across the room.

He grabbed the man nearest him and shoved him toward the door, knocking him off balance. Two men grabbed him from behind. Steve stomped on the foot of the man to his left, hammered him in the groin with his fist and followed through driving his elbow up, catching him full in the chin, then he whirled to face his second attacker who danced out of reach.

"You don't understand!" Carla whimpered. "I'm obligated to them!"

"Bullshit!"

He saw fear in her eyes which fueled his rage.

She slid off the altar and he knocked it over, sending it crashing against the wall. The remains of the group scattered and bolted for the door, most of them half-dressed, except the leader.

"You don't realize the mistake you're making," he said, eyeing Steve with a cold unwavering gaze.

"You're making the mistake, asshole." Steve lunged for him, but Carla got between them.

"No, Steve," she pleaded, shrilly. "You don't know what you're dealing with."

The leader stared at him defiantly until Steve lunged for his throat, grabbing him by the collar of his cape, twisting it until he couldn't breathe. His face turned scarlet and his eyes bulged.

"You'll die for this!" he gasped.

Steve hurled him through the front door and turned to see Carla against the wall clutching the tapestry in a death grip, eyes wide and glazed with fear. She opened her mouth as if to speak, but no words came. Steve fought back a surge of anger and put his fist through the window, shattering it, then he stomped out leaving behind a trampled bouquet and a thin trail of blood leading from the broken window to the door.

The cops found Carla dead the next day from an overdose of opiates.

# CHAPTER THREE

Steve pulled into the lot at work shaking. He parked his bike and wiped tears from his eyes, then took a few tremulous breaths before heading for the door, anxious to lose himself in his work and put his memories out of his mind. He attacked lines of code on his computer and soon lost track of time until his stomach started growling toward the afternoon, so he called in an order for pickup at El Torito's and hopped on his bike.

A young Mexican girl manning the cash register ran his credit card and left to retrieve his order. While waiting he watched an overweight couple with mild amusement. A massive woman with stringy hair and glasses in a faded flower print dress that looked like a shower curtain stuffed her face and reprimanded the man like a marine drill sergeant. The bigger man in a too small Hawaiian shirt that exposed his belly shoveled a taco into his mouth, oblivious to what she said. Beads of sweat stood out on his forehead and his breathing came heavy and labored. The whole time she nagged him, he never once looked up from his plate.

Foodaholics, Steve thought. His judgment felt awkward, then it hit him. They're eating to escape from themselves, but I'm no better. I've been drinking like a fish for the same reason. His realization depressed him until his thoughts were broken by the waitress handing him his food.

After lunch he leaned back in his chair and nodded off, so he went outside, lit a cigarette and inhaled. Nasty habit, he thought, but it'll wake me up. Shit. What the fuck am I going to do tonight? Movie? A dinner? He couldn't face the loneliness. Work kept him occupied, but only for so long. He wanted company, but...

His cell phone rang, interrupting his thoughts. He took it from his pocket and saw it was his work buddy Jaret. Seeing his name brought a sense of relief. A big man with dark hair and a thick mustache, Jaret was good-natured, outgoing, and quick with a wisecrack. He was the first person Steve met when he moved to San Diego. The two of them became good friends in a short period of time and Jaret's wife Amanda was one of the few women Steve could talk to.

"What's up, stud?"

"Hey, big guy." Jaret said. "Why don't you come by for some dinner tomorrow afternoon?"

The invite felt like a lifeline. "Sounds good! What time?"

"That's what I want to hear. See you around four?"

"We're on."

"See you then."

Jaret's invitation lifted his spirits and gave him something to look forward to so he lost himself in his work again until he finished the code he had been working on. After hitting his last keystroke he rubbed his eyes and looked around. Nightfall had come.

Not wanting to repeat his thrill ride of that morning he took his time riding home in darkness and approached the end of I-8 with a growing sense of dread at the prospects of spending the night alone. He reminded himself of Sunday afternoon's home cooked dinner and thought of it as the proverbial light at the end of the tunnel. All he had to do was make it to the end of it.

Saturday night, he thought plopping down on his couch. I feel like going in a million directions and I don't feel like doing anything, but I can't stand to be alone. He looked across the room and spied his two old buddies, Jack Daniels and his guitar. He grabbed the bottle and his Taylor, unscrewed the cap and took a hit that made him feel warm inside, then he took another swig and strummed his guitar, playing and singing, "Captain Jack will get you high tonight," while smoking cigarettes and taking more swigs until he slid into a semi-stupor. The last thing he remembered was another healthy slug from the bottle and looking at his watch. Eleven-forty-five. He took another hit, closed his eyes and put his head back to rest for a second...

He opened them at seven fifteen. His head thundered and morning sunlight streamed through the window. His throat felt raw. The Jack Daniels bottle was still in his hand, and the ashtray on the table in front of him overflowed with butts. Next to it sat a pad of paper that hadn't been there before and beside it the gold pentagram.

His skin crawled, his stomach clenched, and his body went cold like an icy corpse hand had touched the base of his neck. He stared in disbelief for a long puzzling moment.

The note was written in Carla's handwriting. He put the bottle on the table and read it with quivering hands.

**Dear Steve,**

**Words can't express the sorrow and shame I feel for losing you the way I did. I hope to give you some comfort in the knowledge that I am in a better place now and finding my way to blissful happiness. I want you to know that I always loved you, and always will love you. What you saw meant nothing. It was a physical act and nothing more.**

**If you only knew the pain I've suffered. Not a moment goes by that I do not long to be with you again. I should have known that what happened was inevitable. It was a situation I couldn't control. I could not escape from them and I could not bear to be parted from you.**

**I can only hope that you can find the love in your heart to forgive me for causing you the pain you've experienced. My heart is yours forever.**

**All my love, your twin flame,**

**Carla**

He stared at the paper and pendant, unable to think, unable to move. His heart thundered and his stomach tightened, then the print on the page blurred as his tears fell on it.

Someone's playing games – but it's Carla's handwriting – and she's dead.

He stood and shuffled across the room until a wave of nausea threatened.

"God damn it!" he said punctuating the "damn" by slamming his fist against the wall, denting it.

He took two Excedrin, went into his bedroom and lay down face first on the bed before the urge to vomit overcame him.

He barely made it to the bathroom.

He spent an interminable time clutching the toilet and agonizing through dry heaves until he felt reasonably sure they weren't going to return. He took two more Excedrin, crawled back to bed and passed out.

# CHAPTER FOUR

Steve awoke some time after noon with a dry throat and a mild headache that paled in comparison to his morning punishment. After washing down two more Excedrin with a tall glass of cold water he hit the shower which refreshed him. The prospect of spending time with Jaret and Amanda lifted his spirits and took his mind off of the surreal nightmare that met him that morning. He headed North on I-5 and turned off on La Jolla Village Drive for a leisurely cruise up the coast past Torrey Pines and Highway 101 enjoying the fresh ocean breezes.

When he knocked on the door to Jaret's cottage overlooking the beach in Encinitas, the sight of Amanda answering combined with the tantalizing aroma of lasagna overwhelmed him in a multi-sensory embrace. Her sweet loving presence refreshed him more than any breeze from the ocean ever could on levels he rarely felt. More than her beauty, her wholesome energy penetrated him in a mysterious way that he could only think of as love.

"How are you Steve?" She held out her arms and gave him a warm hug that hinted at lavender, melting him to his core, then she stood back and assessed him in a way that made him feel exposed.

"I'm doing okay," he managed.

She gave him a concerned look and graced him with a smile. "Come on in. Jaret's in the kitchen helping out."

She turned and he followed her out to the kitchen. Her petite hour glass body combined with her silky long blonde hair and sparkling green eyes no doubt provided the best advertisement she ever needed for the successful yoga studio she owned in Encinitas. Lucky boy Jaret, he thought.

"Ah, Glass hopper," Jaret said, standing from behind a cutting board, making chopping motions with a big knife. "You rike samurai night fevah?" He glanced over at Amanda, who shook her head in mock disgust.

Jaret set the knife down and wiped his hands on a dish towel before giving Steve a firm handshake, then he pulled him into a hug and patted his back. "Good to see you big guy."

"You too — well not really. It's good to see your sweetheart of a wife." He winked. "You? Well if it weren't for her..."

Amanda smirked and Jaret shook his head. "Yeah, yeah, yeah. That's what they all say." He saluted Amanda and slid the veggies he had chopped off the cutting board into a big bowl. "All set for the salad, boss!"

"Why don't you two take a seat at the table," Amanda said, scooping up the bowl, "and we'll get this show on the road."

Jaret and Steve ate the better part of a small pan of lasagna while Amanda barely ate a thing. After dinner Steve and Jaret sat back contented while Amanda cleared off the table, then on her suggestion they retired to the living room.

"I'm glad to see you haven't lost your appetite," she said, sitting with her legs tucked up under her knees at the other end of the couch from Jaret while Steve relaxed in Jaret's easy chair.

"I don't get to eat like that very often," Steve said patting his stomach. That was awesome. Thank you!"

She smiled. "How are things going Steve? You looked a little off when you came to the door."

He waved it off. "I'm OK. Just having a few little challenges adjusting to my new life out here in Cali, that's all."

"Anything you want to talk about? We're here for you. Anything you need?"

"Got any sisters?"

"Trust me, you don't want to know my sisters, but seriously, anything you want to talk about?"

Yeah, he thought. I keep drinking 'til I black out and waking up to love notes from my dead wife and I keep getting suicidal urges to crash my bike, but other than that... "Thanks, but no, I'm fine. I'm just getting settled in and trying to meet more people."

"What about your life back in Boston?" she said. "You never say much about that."

"Nothing worth talking about!" he said a little too fast and a little too loud.

Amanda blinked like she had been hit and Steve felt bad for being so defensive.

"Sorry." He lowered his voice. "My wife died of an OD and it's a black hole that I don't want to wallow in."

"Sorry, I didn't realize..."

"Don't worry about it." He sat up. "Sorry for snapping. It's something I don't like talking about."

She pursed her lips and nodded. "Understood."

Jaret made chopping motions with his hands. "How's your karate going, Kwai Chang? Make any new friends there?"

"Actually, I did," Steve said brightening at the thought. "Met a kid from Boston who grew up in Dorchester."

"Like Mahky Mahk Wahlberg and his brother Donnie?"

"Yeah. Tough little shit!" Steve felt the beginnings of a smile at the memory of Mick.

"From what I read, Dorchester's a tough place to grow up in," Amanda said. "What's he like? You guys spark up a friendship?"

Steve let his smile come on full. "The little shit spanked my ass!"

"That must have pissed you off, big guy." Jaret nodded, wide-eyed.

"Actually, I didn't mind it at all." Steve shook his head. "He cleaned my clock, but he did it with respect and he stopped by my apartment on the way home and we hung out for a bit."

"Good!" Amanda clapped her hands together. "I'm happy for you."

"We'll see if anything comes of it." *Seeing as I don't remember what we talked about and I don't remember him leaving,* Steve thought. *Hopefully I didn't do anything stupid.* He shrugged. "I'll see him tomorrow night at class."

"I have a good feeling about him," Amanda said. "I think he'll do you some good."

"At this point I can use all the good I can get."

Jaret wiggled his eyebrows. "Any chicks in that class?"

Amanda gave him a little frown.

Steve shook his head. "Stinky, sweaty dudes, that's all."

"Well I wouldn't worry about it right now." Jaret stretched out. "Enjoy your footloose and fancy free lifestyle. You got nobody to worry about but yourself and nobody to answer to. You can be free as the wind with no strings attached and no roots to hold you down."

"Thanks a lot Jaret," Amanda said, pinning him with an indignant look. "I didn't realize I was such a burden."

"That's not what I meant, honey."

"Then what did you mean?, she said, challenging him.

"Single life's not all it's cracked up to be." Steve said, rescuing Jaret. "It has good points and bad points but it gets lonely. Nobody to come home to, nobody to have dinner with, and nobody there when you wake up in the morning."

"Do you think you'll ever get married again?" Amanda asked.

"Right now marriage is the farthest thing from my mind. I doubt if there's anybody who'd put up with me. For that matter, I'm not so sure I want to put up with anybody else."

"Don't worry, Steve," she said softly. "One of these days the right girl will come along. You'll see."

"Right now I'm not going to worry about it." Right now I'm fucking loony tunes, he thought. "I'm going to go on alone so I can get my act together."

An awkward silence fell over them until Amanda said, "I think it's time for dessert."

# CHAPTER FIVE

Steve woke up Monday morning remembering fragments of a dream about being with Carla and something about them being twin flames. The unpleasant memory of Saturday night's black out and the puzzling letter that greeted him on Sunday morning amplified his fears and lingered throughout the day casting a pall over everything. He could barely drag himself out of bed.

Getting motivated at work was an added challenge, but toward afternoon he started thinking about conditioning class at the karate studio that night. He half looked forward to it and half dreaded it. He needed the discipline and hoped to talk with Mick again, hoping he hadn't said or done anything stupid in his blackout after their last class.

When five o'clock came he headed straight for the studio and parked his bike in the alley. He felt a little apprehensive walking in through the back door embracing the distinct smell that came from years of sweat and hard work.

Smokey, their sensei stood at the front of the studio with his arms crossed, nodding to acknowledge Steve as he entered. Tall and brown-skinned, Smokey had a lean muscular build and moved light on his feet like a cat, speaking softly while teaching a private lesson while others practiced kicks, punches, and self defense techniques in front of mirrors lining two facing walls. Others stretched on the floor. Smokey's presence had a way of charging the atmosphere with authority.

Steve heard his measured voice through the wall of the dressing room while putting on his gi.

"You have to learn to be centered and balanced at all times. Not just your physical center, but your spiritual and mental centers as well and you have to stay in the moment instead of being emotional and lost in your thoughts. Be in the here and now. Right now. That is the secret to being an effective martial artist."

Steve came out and spied Mick stretching in the corner, so he bowed at the edge of the carpet showing his respect and sat next to Mick to do his own stretches. Mick nodded and winked, but didn't say anything out of respect for the lesson in progress. His friendly greeting put Steve at ease, assuring him that he hadn't said or done anything stupid in his black out.

Smokey finished the private lesson and walked to the back of the studio saying, "Let's put our shoes on and get in a good run."

Everyone filed into the alley and did last minute stretches until Smokey came out, locked the door, and headed off running down the alley, students trailing. He led them down to the beach and put them to work plodding through soft sand and running backward. The longer they went, the more Steve dropped behind gasping for air, his lungs on fire. He thought about quitting until Mick dropped back.

"Come on, Steve. We've got to show these guys that Boston homies are tough."

Steve struggled along wheezing for air, fighting an upset stomach. Finally he stopped. "My lungs are killing me," he managed between gasps, "and my legs feel like lead."

"You getting too old for this or are you just turning into a sissy?" Mick taunted, "or maybe those nasty ass cancer sticks aren't worth it."

"You're right." He started running again. "No excuse."

"That's the spirit!"

Smokey took them back to the studio to finish the workout. Along one wall three guys did sit ups, at another three did knuckle push ups, three more did jumping jacks by the third, and along the last wall one worked a speed bag, one worked a heavy bag, and the last one did twenty-five wheel kicks on a heavy bag with each leg yelling "Kee-yeah!" with the last kick, signaling everyone to rotate to the next spot until they completed the circuit.

I'll never touch another cigarette, Steve thought lying flat on his back after it was over suppressing the urge to vomit.

Feeling defeated and incoherent he skulked out of the studio before anyone noticed, dragged himself home and crawled into a hot bath struggling with the urge for a cigarette before giving in. The smoke hurt his lungs and made his throat raw, but calmed him more with each inhalation. Strange, he thought. This whole process is a little bit of death in itself. Here I am destroying myself after a healthy workout.

On Wednesday he pushed past his trepidation and showed up for sparring class and his private lesson from John, a lanky, dark curly-haired brown belt. When his session with John ended Smokey came out of his office. "Okay," he said. "Line up according to rank. Upper belts in the front, lower belts to the rear."

Steve took his place at the back and the class bowed to Smokey with their left hands covering their right fists before Smokey took them through a series of warm ups and stretches. "All right, Smokey said when they finished. "Everyone put on your safety gear." The group donned boxing gloves, shin guards, and sparring shoes, and sat around the edge of the carpet.

Steve watched upper belts spar in spirited matches with a mixture of admiration and apprehension. His first opponent was another beginner named Chris, a thin, curly purple-haired punk rocker orange belt with a diamond stud in his ear. After bowing to each other with their left hands over their right fists they had a brisk match scoring pretty evenly on each other. Steve felt good, but out of breath. Bowing out he turned to take his seat, but Smokey stopped him and matched him against John.

They bowed to each other and John went to work on Steve's head and body with combination punches and a flurry of kicks that left Steve frustrated and more out of breath. He tried desperately to score on John without success. At the moment he thought he might pass out Smokey stopped the match.

Relieved, Steve went to sit down and Smokey stopped him again. This time Steve found himself face to face with Mick who winked as he bowed, then blitzed in on Steve, taking advantage of the fact that he was winded. Steve tried to put up a fight but found it impossible. His arms burned and his ribs ached so he backed off and bent over, gasping for air.

"Need a second to catch my breath," he said between wheezes.

"If you were in a street situation, nobody would stop and give you a breather," Smokey said, then to Mick. "Get on him!"

Mick zeroed in on Steve's stomach. Steve sensed him pulling his punches and had all he could do to keep his arms up. Finally, after minutes that seemed like hours, Smokey stopped the match.

"You tired Steve?"

"No."

"Good. Take a seat."

Steve sat down lightheaded and nauseous to watch the rest of the class spar, thankful Smokey didn't call on him to fight again.

After class when everyone went back to the dressing room Mick sidled up to Steve.

"Hope I didn't give you too bad a time," he said, "but I had no choice. It's for your own good."

"You don't have to apologize. I know you had to do that better than anybody."

"Glad to hear it. You got any plans for the weekend?"

Steve thought about work but answered, "Not really."

"What do you say we take our Harley's out to the mountains? I know some good roads."

"You ride?"

Mick rolled his eyes in an exaggerated gesture.

Steve smiled. "Sounds great!"

# CHAPTER SIX

Saturday turned out beautiful with warm weather and a clear sky. Mick led them East on I-8 past El Cajon where the highway began a steady incline that grew steeper as they went until they pulled off at the Sunrise Highway exit and stopped at the end of the ramp.

"This is where it gets good," Mick called out over the rumble of their engines. He gave Steve a mischievous smirk and took off on a twisting road with Steve trailing through a series of rocky passes where they stood on their foot pegs from time to time to admire the view. As they rode higher into the mountains the trees became thicker. After weaving along a series of small pine groves, sucking in the crisp tang of the cool, pine-scented air Mick signaled Steve to follow him off the highway onto a dirt fire road through woods that ended at a cliff.

Mick killed his engine, took off his helmet and put down his kickstand. "This is my favorite spot." He smiled and held his arms out. "I think of it as my power spot." He pointed. "Check out that view."

They overlooked a large pine filled valley surrounded by mountain peaks. The mid-day sun cast shades of purple and grays between jagged peaks and pines studded the mountain sides in thick growths.

"I see why you like it," Steve said. "It's inspiring."

"That it is!" Mick wandered over to a bed of pine needles and Steve followed, taking a seat beside him. A soft wind blew and a blue jay hopped up onto a branch squawking at a squirrel nibbling on a pine cone. The squirrel chittered back its disapproval.

They sat without speaking for a long time drinking in the scenery and enjoying the solitude until Steve's inner turmoil bubbled to the surface.

"Hey, Mick, you got a girl friend."

Mick shook his head. "Not at present."

"How do you deal with loneliness? You live by yourself, don't drink, don't smoke, or hang out in bars chasing girls. I get the feeling you've kind of separated yourself from the rest of the world."

Mick chuckled. "I've had my share of drunk chicks and drama. Without coming across as judgmental, to be honest, I have no use for alcohol. In my experience all it does is make people dull, stupid sounding, and boring, even though they might think they are the life of the party. Either they're happy drunks or they get mean and they tend to repeat themselves and slur their words. Half the time you can't understand a word they say. Fuck that!"

"They turn into completely different people, don't they?"

"I don't think it has any basis in truth, but I read somewhere that the word alcohol comes from an Arabic word Alkhul or something like that that means body eating spirit and is supposedly the origin of the word ghoul."

Mick's words hit Steve in the heart like a knife and he felt himself choke up a little.

"Don't get me wrong," Mick added. "I don't mind if people want to drink and blow off a little steam from time to time, and I don't care if they get drunk every once in awhile. Shit, it's a major part of our culture, so I tolerate it, but I do my best to avoid it." He spread his arms out again as if embracing the whole valley. "*This* is what gets me high."

Steve fumbled for a cigarette. "Don't you crave female company?"

"Sure! Sometimes I get lonely, but lately I've been happier and more at peace being alone and right now that's okay for me. I love women, but I don't always crave their company, not in the way you think. Maybe someday the right one will come along, but I don't feel like I need one. That's why I think I can genuinely love one."

Steve held up his hands in surrender. "I don't know how to deal with my emptiness. It's like part of me is missing."

Mick gazed out into the valley as if weighing his words. Steve found his attitude both puzzling and strangely comforting.

"There's a big difference between need and love," Mick continued. "I went looking for love from women, but literally in all the wrong places like bars, booze, and dope..." He paused, then, "Well the dope thing isn't so cut and dried, but I realized that I couldn't find love in any of those escapes. How could I find love in a relationship if I wasn't bringing any to it? Too many people go into relationships taking, and if they do give, for the most part they have an agenda, and what they think of as love is really use, then the relationship turns into a contest to see who can out-use who. Smokey says, 'Each one tries to have without being had in the process of having.' It's a no win situation. Is that what happened with Carla?"

Steve bit back his response. How the fuck did he know about Carla? His mind spun in a flurry of disjointed thoughts, images, and emotions to the first night they hung out, but he couldn't remember anything definitive and had no memory of talking about Carla. His mental abyss put him on edge making him feel trapped, so he simply shook his head.

"Sorry," Mick said. "Didn't mean to pry, but you talked about her a lot the other night, so if you're not comfortable talking about it now don't worry."

Steve grasped for something to say, feeling like he had lost the thread of conversation in the darkness of that night and couldn't find his way back, so he grasped for a new direction. "What do you mean about the dope thing not being cut and dried? Booze, drugs, they're just different ways of escaping, aren't they?"

"Well-- yes and no."

"What does that mean? Sounds like a contradiction to me."

Mick took a deep breath and let it out, then looked Steve in the eye. "It all comes down to intention."

"Intention?"

Mick nodded. "When I was a kid, my motto was try as many new things as you can and believe me I did. Drinking, sniffing glue, weed, acid, mushrooms, speed, downers. You name it I tried it, sometimes more than once." He chuckled. "Sometimes a lot more than once, but I had no method to my madness, no direction, and no guidance. I was a walking science fair experiment, but I got bored with drinking and saw what it did to everyone around me and decided that in many ways it was worse than cocaine or heroin because it was socially acceptable and easy to get. More than that I realized that alcohol, heroin, and other shit along those lines depressed me, closed me off, and made me stupid. All they did was give me the illusion of shutting out the world, but I always woke up the next morning feeling like shit and my problems were still there, maybe even worse than before. All I wanted was that next drink or I was jonesing for the next buzz, whatever form that took."

Steve realized he was nodding. "Ain't that the truth."

"So I came to the conclusion that those things shut you down and stifle your perception and awareness. On the other hand I discovered that psychedelics like magic mushrooms and LSD used in the right way with the right respect could open you up and expand your perception instead of deadening it. I was struggling with the whole thing until I read a book called Food of the Gods by Terence McKenna that made me aware of the fact that psychedelic plants have been used since prehistoric times for spiritual purposes to expand consciousness, not deaden it."

"Isn't LSD a chemical?"

"LSD comes from a fungus and mushrooms are a fungus," but as strong as they can be, they pale in comparison to the strongest plant medicine of all, Ayahuasca."

"Ayawhatsca?"

"Ayahuasca."

"What about all the bad trip stuff you always hear about?"

Mick gave a dismissive wave. "That's mostly bullshit. There's really no such thing as a bad trip. Even if it is experienced as a bad trip, in the end it's a good one. People mistakenly think that because they have a dark experience that they have taken a harmful substance, but in reality what is perceived of as bad and negative originates inside of them and the negative release they experience is the repressed shadow trauma they have been denying coming to the surface. Handled properly in the right context they can let it go and free themselves of it which ultimately adds to a better sense of well being and self respect."

"A bad trip is a good trip? I need to think about that one."

"They call these plant medicines entheogens. Theo is the Latin root for God, so it basically means the God within the plant that brings out the God within you. It's called food of the gods, or what ancient cultures revered as the flesh of the gods that open you up, making you expansive, opening up Pandora's Box if you will, letting out the hidden good and bad. If you have the fortitude to stay on the path they will eventually force you to face your demons."

The word demon sent a shiver through Steve followed by a flurry of dark images, sensations, and emotions that ended with a spinning loop of the last time he saw Carla alive when he had walked in on the satanic ceremony that she had been the center of.

The flicker of candlelight through the curtains. The altar in the living room. The gold pentagram with the inverted crucifix. Carla's friends naked and paired off in male-female pairs. The low murmur of their chants droning "Say-tan. Say-tan." Carla nude on the altar. The hooded black man prepared to mount her.

"Steve!" Mick said, bringing him back. "You okay?"

He gave a quick shake of his head, still feeling the chill. "I don't think I'm ready for that."

Mick nodded. "You're not. I'll save it for another time if you want to learn more. I may have told you too much already. Most people don't know this side of me." He pointed across the valley to where the sky darkened with approaching storm clouds and stood. "We better get going. Maybe we can outrun it."

They got back on their bikes and headed down the mountain roads. By the time they hit the freeway large rain drops forced them to slow down. When they reached San Diego Mick pulled up alongside Steve and signaled that he was going his own way.

Back in his apartment Steve found himself alone with his thoughts and a deep yearning to understand how to deal with the dark emptiness Carla had left him with.

# CHAPTER SEVEN

Steve heard noise by his office door, looked up, and Jaret's head popped in.

"Hey, big guy, what are you doing this weekend?"

"I was thinking about rattling my buddy Mick and taking a bike ride through the mountains to clear my head."

"You called him yet?"

"No."

Jaret smiled mischievously. "Ever been to Vegas?"

"No." The thought of it appealed to his sense of adventure. It *was* something to check off his bucket list, but another part of him...

"Never? I'm going with my buddy Jon to blow off some steam. Why don't you come with us?"

"What about Amanda?"

"She's visiting her mother and this is one of the few chances I'll get to play."

In spite of his trepidation the prospect of a weekend full of distractions might be just what he needed to take his mind off of things. He threw up his arms. "What the hell, why not?"

Short, with a medium build, Jon had curly dirty blonde hair and wild blue eyes. He sat in the front seat of his BMW with Jaret and Steve sat in the back. Once on the road out of town Jon pulled out a joint and passed it around. When they finished he caught Steve's attention in the rear view mirror and dramatically wiggled his eyebrows like a cartoon villain, then Tom Petty's Free Fallin' blasted through the car. Steve and

Jaret both jumped and Jon's eyes widened in exaggerated shock, sending Steve into hysterics in his first laugh in months. Jon and Jaret cracked up along with him until Steve caught his breath with tears rolling down his cheeks.

"Sorry man," Jon said, "but Free Fallin's kind of my theme song."

Their humorous jump start set the tone for their drive to Vegas smoking pot, listening to music, and talking about hot chicks and the pleasures of sin city.

Jon played Free Fallin' again when they pulled into the parking lot at Caesar's Palace. Once parked, he pulled out a small mirror, poured out a small pile of cocaine and made three neat lines side by side. Smiling, he handed Steve a rolled up hundred dollar bill. Steve looked up at the expectant faces of Jon and Jaret and put the bill to one nostril. Pressing the other one shut he snorted. It burned when it hit his nose. He felt the coke sticking to the back of his throat numbing it as his heart raced and a rush of euphoria filled him. He looked up at Jon and Jaret, smiled and handed them the mirror. They looked at each other and smiled back before snorting their respective rails.

They walked into a cacophony of flashing lights, ringing chimes, bells, beeps, and other electronic alarms from slots at Caesar's. Scantily clad waitresses ran to and fro with trays of drinks. Steve felt a strong pull at his solar plexus, the same sensation he felt as a kid when he was scared, only subtler, like some kind of warning, then an odd feeling shot through him like he was two separate people, one of them excited, the other threatened. An image of a cartoon angel floating by his right shoulder and a cartoon devil floating on his left popped into his head.

An X-rated playground, he thought. Disneyland for grownups. No, more like fucking Sodom and Gomorrah!

Jaret's voice shook him out of it above the din of everything.

"I don't know about you, Steve, but I'm going to check out some black jack. What about you, Jon?"

"I'm going to the bar. Who knows? Maybe I'll fall in love."

"I'm going to take a look around," Steve said, "I'll hook up with you guys later."

Jon headed off into the crowd while Jaret gravitated to the nearest blackjack table. Steve walked through a sprawling maze of slot machines with flashing lights, electronic sounds and music, and frantic colorful video displays. Little gray-haired grannies, beautiful young ladies dressed to kill, black, white, Asian, middle eastern, young, old, fat, tall, skinny, sitting quietly, entirely focused on the task at hand or shouting in triumph and disgust.

As the noise of the slots faded behind him, he headed into a sea of gaming tables where the floor was covered with thick, plush, carpets. Huge mirrors covered the ceiling and the sound of a band spilled out of a lounge punctuated by the voices of dealers calling out numbers. Rich people won and lost thousands of dollars at a time looked bored and resigned while those of lesser fortune were animated, desperately trying to make that one lucky bet.

With all its flash and people, a carnival atmosphere reigned and underneath that Steve's impression sank from carnival to carnal. His heart still raced, so he went outside and walked around the parking lot to smoke some weed to take the edge off his cocaine high, then he went back and found Jaret and Jon at a blackjack table where the three of them spent the better part of the night playing blackjack until their enthusiasm waned around three in the morning. Steve went to his room and crawled into bed instantly falling fast asleep.

He awoke to the sound of knocking. When he realized it wasn't going to stop he rolled out of bed and answered it. Jon and Jaret came bounding into the room with a tray.

"What time is it?" Steve asked, climbing back into bed.

"Nine o'clock in the morning," Jon answered. "We brought room service."

Steve rolled over and looked at them, then at the tray with a huge line of coke and a shot of whiskey on it.

"Oh God," he mumbled and sat up mechanically to take his 'medicine'.

After smoking a joint with them he showered and they spent the better part of the day playing black jack, drinking, and sneaking back to their rooms for rails of coke and tokes of weed until early evening when they felt hungry.

They walked out into the hot night air and looked up and down the strip. Its multicolored, flashing neon lights had a strobing effect that gave the strip a life of its own. They found a restaurant just off the main drag and ordered a big meal. Although none of them ate more than half of what they ordered the food had a welcome grounding effect.

Steve couldn't help but notice the hookers when he walked back in through the bar at Caesar's and they made it a point to notice him. He felt an urge to check one out, but didn't want to do anything in front of Jaret. He looked over at Jon and their eyes met, telling him that Jon had the same thoughts. Following Jaret, they went back into the casino and began playing for bigger stakes. As soon as they started getting too drunk, they slipped away for snorts of coke and hits of pot. When midnight rolled around they were all drunk, especially Jaret who could barely walk.

Jon and Steve helped him back to his room and put him to bed for the night and went back to the casino.

"What do you want to do now?" Steve said when they walked in.

Jon smiled and his eyes sparkled. "You know."

As soon as they went into a bar two hookers sitting together in a booth looked them over and gave them a wide-eyed inviting look. One of the girls had long blonde hair and tight blue satin pants. Her friend had long, curly red tresses, large gold earrings, and a striking red frilly blouse that showed world class cleavage.

"You guys looking for a little company?" the blonde asked.

"Sure are," Jon answered.

Steve smiled, suddenly feeling embarrassed.

"Okay then." Jon rubbed his hands. "What do you say we have a drink to get to know each other a little better?"

They sat together making small talk for awhile before Jon and the blonde slipped away leaving Steve with the red head, who seemed a little tipsy. As if to confirm it, she ordered a third Margarita. For some strange reason Steve thought about Carla which made him uneasy. He wished he hadn't gotten himself into his predicament.

His red-headed model gorgeous companion noticed his awkwardness and slid closer to him, whispering in his ear with hot moist breath. "It's okay, babe." She stroked his inner thigh, arousing him. "Relax, I'm not going to bite."

Her warm presence and intoxicating perfume overwhelmed him and her eyes reminded him of Carla's. A diminishing part of him wanted to get away, but the pleasure continued to build until he couldn't suppress himself any longer. "Let's do it," he said, feeling as if someone else spoke through him.

They went up to his room and each did a line of coke that Jon had left on a tray.

"Listen honey," the red head said wiping her nose. "This blow is real fine, but it's going to cost you five hundred bills to get this party in gear. Can you swing it?"

Steve stared at her a moment, startled by her frankness.

"I don't have that much cash," he mumbled.

"No worries." She pulled an iPhone from her purse. "Credit card is fine." She looked directly at him, all business. He fumbled his card from his wallet and watched her punch in the number before signing it with his finger. She handed him back his card, put the phone back in her purse and in a few minutes time she had them both undressed and in bed. After clinically efficient sex she went into the bathroom and dressed herself, then left looking picture perfect. Scarcely twenty minutes had passed.

It happened so quickly, Steve found himself drifting into a mild state of shock. He lit a cigarette and lay back in bed feeling guilty. Strictly sex. No emotion. Cold and professional. It felt like she took part of him with her, leaving him drained. He snuffed out his cigarette thinking how it felt sordid and loveless. He had paid for the use of her body like he paid for a rental car, only he was the one who felt used.

With that thought he drifted off into a fitful slumber and woke up around eight-thirty the next morning with a dull headache, a dry throat, and a worn out depleted feeling. He took two Excedrin and went into the bathroom.

The same satanic symbols he had seen at Carla's "mass" were scrawled on the mirror with bright red lipstick in Carla's handwriting. Beneath them in large letters were the words:

"Psalm 89 Verse 48."

The sight of it jolted him and made his heart slam in his chest like he had been punched. His attention shot to the toilet where the Gideon Bible lay submerged in the bottom. He fished it out and sat down on the tile floor, gingerly leafing through the dripping pages until he came to Psalm 89, verse 48.

**What man is he that liveth, and shall not see death? Shall he deliver his soul from the hand of the grave? Se'lah.**

He stared at the verse knowing what happened, but couldn't bring himself to face it. He stood and let the book fall to the floor and with a sinking feeling mechanically cleaned off the mirror before burying the water-soaked Bible in the trash basket.

After showering he sat in one of the hotel's restaurants staring into the blackness of his coffee. Being in Vegas made him feel as if he was not in control of himself more than any other place he had ever been. He never would have brought a hooker home under normal circumstances. It felt like booze, drugs, and solicited sex were more than he could handle. He realized that Vegas had a way of making you conform to its hedonistic way of life. The more you got, the more you wanted, but the more you wanted, the more *they* got.

"There he is!" He heard Jon say from behind him.

Jaret and Jon sat on either side of him. "We figured you'd be here."

"You guys look like shit, just like I feel," Steve mumbled.

"You ain't exactly looking beautiful yourself," Jon countered.

"What do you say we have a little breakfast and make a last run on the casino before we head home?" Jaret caught the waitresses' eye and held up his finger.

Steve sipped his coffee, not wanting to show his real feelings. "I'll tell you what. No matter how much money we've got, and no matter how we feel, let's set a six o'clock deadline. How's that sound?"

Jaret nodded. "That'll get us back to San Diego around midnight."

By six o'clock, Jaret had lost around two hundred and fifty dollars and Jon lost about forty while Steve broke even. When they pulled up to Jaret's some time after midnight Steve's heart sank when he saw his bike on its side with its front wheel and forks bent and twisted. He stormed over to it burning with rage and found an envelope taped to the gas tank. He tore it off and ripped it open.

To the owner of this motorcycle,

I'm so sorry for backing into your motorcycle. I was driving a U-Haul and didn't see it. I should have been paying more attention to what I was doing. I asked around the neighborhood, but nobody knew who owned it. Please contact me at 619- 555-4040 and we can make things right. I have already talked to my insurance agent and my coverage will take care of everything.

Please don't be angry.

Heather Foley

# CHAPTER EIGHT

Steve stood outside a cottage two doors down from Jaret and Amanda's struggling with his rage. He went to knock and hesitated, then took a deep breath, let it out slowly, and knocked with a speech forming in his mind. The door opened and no words came when he looked into the clearest turquoise eyes he had ever seen. She gazed back at him for a long moment before looking away and breaking the silence.

"You must be here about the motorcycle."

Petite and willowy with graceful curves, she wore light blue shorts revealing long legs and a lavender halter top. Long silky blonde hair hung over her shoulders. She had a tangible innocence and a delicate beauty that brought images of hummingbirds to mind.

"That's right," he almost whispered.

"Please come in," she said softly. "I'm Heather. I'm so sorry about your motorcycle." Her voice sounded like a cross between tinkling wind chimes and the sound of gentle trickling water.

Tinkerbell, he thought.

She beckoned him in and Steve's heart made a little jump when he saw no ring on her left hand.

"I didn't even see it," she continued. "I'm so embarrassed. I'm not used to driving big trucks..."

"Whoa!" Steve held up his hands. "It's all right. Your insurance is going to cover it, right?"

She nodded. "I'm expecting a call back from my agent any minute now. Can I get you a cup of coffee or something?"

"Coffee's fine, and don't worry about the bike. Everything will work out." She could have backed over *me* and I'd still forgive her, he thought as he followed the sweet hint of nectar from whatever perfume she wore through a room of furniture, stacked boxes, framed pictures and art into a kitchen full of partially unpacked boxes.

"How do you like your coffee?" she said pouring two cups.

"Black is fine."

"I feel terrible about hitting your motorcycle," She said joining him at the table. "I hope I can make up for any inconvenience I've caused you." She blushed a little and lowered her eyes. "I just moved here from Michigan a few weeks ago. I don't know a soul."

"Well you do now, although I could think of easier ways to meet people." He stifled a grin. "Seriously though, it was thoughtful of you to leave the note on my bike. You could have taken off."

She glanced up and shook her head. "I couldn't live with myself. I knocked on doors to find out who owned your bike, but nobody knew"

"I was out of town with my buddy Jaret who lives two doors down."

Her cell phone rang from the other room and she jumped up to answer. Steve felt a deep longing watching the last of her tanned slender legs disappear out the door. After talking for a few minutes she came back excited. "That was my insurance agent. He gave me the number of a towing company to call and the address of a place to take your motorcycle. I also have the name of a car rental agency that will rent you a car until your motorcycle is fixed." She clapped her hands together. "And they're footing the whole bill."

"That's great!"

Heather called the towing company and gave him a ride to the car rental agency.

"Are you doing anything Friday night?" He asked when she pulled into the car rental lot.

She looked a little surprised. "I didn't have any plans."

"Seeing as you feel so bad about running over my bike, I'm feeling magnanimous and decided to let you make it up to me by letting me take you out to dinner."

She giggled, wind chimes and water, and looked over at him. Their eyes met for another small eternity, then they both turned away.

"I've got a better idea," she said after an awkward silence. "Why don't I cook you dinner? That's the least I can do. Friday night? Seven?"

He held up a finger. "Sold!"

He left work in a hurry on Friday and as it drew closer to seven his excitement turned to nervousness. His thoughts had been filled with her sweetness all week; the sparkle in her eyes, the way she moved, the gentle caress of her voice, her perfume, but on his drive North the specter of Carla made him edgy, especially in light of his blackouts. No way I'm getting shitfaced tonight, he resolved to himself. No fucking way!

He felt strangely guilty for seeing Heather as if he were being unfaithful, but Carla was gone and he had to get on with his life.

He stopped by a flower stand in Encinitas and picked up a bouquet, then rushed to Heather's. His heart beat quickened when he walked up to the front door and his anticipation grew. He hid the flowers behind his back and rang the bell.

She looked radiant in a frilly aqua colored blouse that accented the magic of her turquoise eyes and faded jeans that hugged her curves. Steve found himself a little tongue-tied. He pulled out the flowers.

Her eyes grew big. "Thank you, Steve! That's sweet of you. You didn't have to do that. They're beautiful."

"Pretty flowers for a pretty lady."

"Come on in." She smiled all the way up through her eyes.

A pleasant aroma wafted from the kitchen as he walked in behind her. The pictures and art work had been hung and the living room was impeccably arranged and tastefully decorated with feminine nick-knacks and brightly colored Persian carpets.

"Hey good lookin', what ya got cookin'?"

"Chicken Kiev," she said. "My mom's recipe. I hope you like it." She nodded toward the couch. "Make yourself at home while I put these in some water."

Steve took a seat and was hit with an intrusive rush of memories of Carla. He brushed them off when Heather came back arranging the flowers in a vase. She set it on the coffee table in front of him and took a seat on the other end of the couch.

"What do you do for a living?"

"I'm a systems analyst," he said, feeling like Carla was in the room with them. "What about you?"

"I have my Master's in marine biology and moved here a few weeks ago to take a job at Scripps Institution of Oceanography to study whales. Michigan isn't exactly a marine biologist's paradise, so San Diego was the place to be. What about you? Your accent tells me you're not from here either."

"I'm from Boston. I pahk my cah in Havahd yahd."

She giggled and its light-hearted musicality reminded him of hummingbirds. Tinkerbell, he thought again.

"I've only been out here a few weeks myself," she said.

"How do you like it so far?"

"Love it."

She held her hands together, then smiling and nodding said, "I think dinner's ready."

Steve stood when she got up. "Need any help?"

"I have everything under control."

They had a quiet candlelit dinner, with wine and soft music. After dinner they went back to the living room and sat on the couch a little closer together than before.

Heather handed him a glass of wine. "Have you ever been married?"

His hand jumped, spilling wine on the carpet. "Shit, I'm sorry."

"Don't worry about it." She hustled out to the kitchen and came back with carpet cleaner and a sponge. After mopping up the spill she came back and rejoined him. "Good as new!"

He stared at the floor. "I was married once, but not for very long. I'm widowed now."

"I can tell it's painful to talk about," Heather said. "Let's change the subject.

They talked long into the night and the more Steve felt drawn to her the more uneasy he felt about Carla whose "presence" kept forcing itself into his mind until he had a headache and couldn't think straight.

"I'd better get going." He rubbed his eyes, "It's five in the morning. Otherwise I'll stay forever."

Heather looked a little disappointed. "You can stay if you want." She stood. "You can sleep on the couch."

He wanted to but his unease about Carla coupled with his fear of having another of his horrific nightmares held him back — and he had drank a few glasses of wine. "I really should get going and let you get some sleep, but can I take you out to dinner tonight?"

"Okay," she said, gracing him with a smile that he thought could launch far more than a thousand ships.

# CHAPTER NINE

"Heather's brought about a total change in my life," Steve said after he killed his engine, put his kickstand down, and took off his helmet. "When I'm with her I don't drink much, but I still drink and once I get going I have a tendency to go overboard."

Mick nodded, walking toward his his "power spot" in the pine needles by the cliff overlooking the valley. He sat down in his usual place. "Your problem is more than drinking."

"How do you know that?"

"From the way you act."

Steve dropped down beside him and looked out over the valley. It was late afternoon and the weather had cooled. The sun hung low on the horizon and the wild life around them chirped, twittered, and buzzed as if announcing the spectacular show the sunset was about to give them.

"My ex...", Steve struggled to find the words, then "My ex wife..." He hit another blank spot then a torrent of words came. "She's been a curse to me in more ways than one." He clenched his fist. "That's when I started having problems with getting high. Before that I could take it or leave it, but now it has me by the balls. No matter how hard I try, I can't seem to free myself. Heather's the best thing that's happened to me and I don't want to fuck that up but – Carla's been dead for some time now..."

Mick gave him a sideways glance. "Carla? I didn't realize she had died."

"It's not something I talk about and the last thing I want is a pity party."

"You don't have to worry about that from me, that's for sure, but I did have my suspicions."

"But you never said anything?"

"I don't like to pry. You said a lot when we first met, but other than that you've pretty much kept it in. I figured you'd tell me what was on your mind when you were ready."

"Part of me still feels connected to Carla in a way I can't understand. It feels like she's fucking haunting me. I mean *haunting* me. It's more than just nightmares and bad memories. It's stronger like it's – don't get me wrong. I'm absolutely stone cold crazy about Heather, but I still feel empty in the weirdest way, even when I'm with her. Like a piece of me is lost and something else is driving me to drinking and drugs." Steve took out a cigarette and lit it. "It's not fair to Heather. I spend every spare minute with her and it feels like I can't get enough of her, but – I'd swear that weird guilty Carla feeling gets stronger when I'm with Heather and when I'm not with her I'm driven back to getting high even more. It's maddening!"

"Listen, partner." Mick patted him on the shoulder. "You're not going to solve all your problems overnight. These things take time. I'll help you, but you have to help me help you."

Steve sighed. "My whole life revolves around Heather. Carla's gone. I can't help myself. I feel like I need Heather and I want more than anything to devote myself fully to her, but that missing feeling..."

"Give yourself some time to get your head clear and don't beat yourself up. I promise I'll help you find clarity. The first thing you need to do is get off the booze, the weed, and anything else that alters you."

"What about those plant medicines you mentioned. What did you call them? Ayawhootska and entheogens."

"Ayahuasca. Yeah, that's what I'm talking about."

"You said that if I had the fortitude to stay on the path it would force me to face my demons."

Mick nodded sagely. "It's not something to take lightly. You need to get clear before you can do that. You have to approach it with the utmost respect which means purifying yourself to put your body into kind of a chemically pure state, then you have to follow a special cleansing diet at least a week before you take it."

Steve smacked his fist into his palm. "I'm going to do it! I'll do whatever it takes to get free of this shit."

Mick studied him for a moment and seemed to come to some kind of decision. "Just promise you'll be careful and go gentle on yourself. I'm a little worried about you. If you find yourself in a spot I'm just a phone call away."

"Thanks bro, I appreciate that."

The blazing red fire of the sun hit the horizon and nightfall approached. The sounds of birds, bugs, and other animals diminished and stars popped out in the coming darkness.

"This is the time between the worlds," Mick said in hushed tones, "one of the two most powerful times of the day." He pointed. "It marks the death of the day."

"And the birth of the night," Steve added.

Later that week Heather left for a whale study expedition on a Scripps research vessel. Steve decided that the week of her absence would give him a jump start on cleaning up his act so that any weirdness and withdrawals he might go through would happen out of her sight. Without his usual distractions he did everything he could to keep himself occupied. He smoked weed for the first couple of days and went the next couple of days without it until he found himself sitting on his couch on Friday night with the jitters, wringing his hands thinking, I need a drink. Can't. Have to. No! I made it this far. I'm going the distance.

He breathed in and out trying to shake the nervous energy that filled him, but it seemed to build, making him feel wild and compulsive. He jumped when the phone rang.

"Hello?"

"Steve?"

"Yeah."

"Hey bud, it's Jon. Where you been keeping yourself?"

"Spending time with Heather."

"Can't say I blame you. You're lucky you met her first. Man oh man is she a goddess!" He chuckled. "I'd eat a mile of her shit just to kiss her ass."

Steve snorted. "You can kiss mine!"

"Grow some tits and maybe I'll think about it." Jon chuckled again. "Listen, Jaret told me she's out of town. Why don't you come down from your ivory tower and rub elbows with us lower class slobs? I'm having a little get together tonight."

Steve realized that his hand holding the phone shook. "I don't know, Jon. I don't think I'm in the mood..."

"Don't be a spoilsport. Jaret and Amanda are coming."

"I don't know..."

"You can always come and if you don't want to stick around you can leave. I'll understand, but at least make an appearance. We love and miss you, bro, and we haven't seen you for awhile."

Steve sighed. He couldn't stand being alone. Maybe some socializing would do him some good. Take the edge off of things. "Well — okay."

He hit the end call icon on his cell screen and wiped his sweaty palms on his pants. Fuck it! I need a shot to loosen up before I go."

He poured it with shaking hands and its warmth soothed him.

Jon answered the door wearing a fedora with a big owl feather sticking up from the hat band greeting Steve with a mixture of Carlos Santana, reefer, and the sound of the party from the crowded room behind him. "Hey Steve! Glad you could make it."

"Me too."

"You look like you got a little head start on the rest of us. How about a little something to pick you up?"

He did feel a little tipsy. Maybe a little bump of coke would bring him back some. "Sounds good."

"Step into my office and we'll see what the doctor has to offer." He led Steve through the crowd into his bedroom and produced a small mirror with a bunch of rails neatly laid out on one side.

"I can see you've been busy." Steve took a small straw from Jon.

Jon smiled. "Have a blast. In fact have two."

"Thanks." Fuck it! Steve put the straw to his nose and snorted both lines. The coke burned when it hit, his heart and thoughts accelerated, and his head cleared. Numbness followed. Just what he needed.

Jon took the straw, snorted a bump himself and put the mirror away.

"Just like the good times in Vegas." He wiped his nose with the back of his hand and patted Steve on the back. "Good to see you, bro. Thanks for coming!"

Steve followed him back to the front room where he took a few hits of weed from a pipe and mingled with the crowd. Smoking ganja took the edge off his "buzz" and relaxed him more. He slouched back in a corner chair, closed his eyes for a bit, and lost himself in the music, identifying with each song, letting it carry him through a range of emotions. He smiled, reliving memories of playing with Butch and Charlie back in the Triple Threat days until he heard Jaret's voice. "Hey dude! What are you doing, contemplating the universe?"

"No, man, just getting into some old tunes."

He stood and gave Amanda a hug, feeling comfort in her warmth. "How's it going, sweetheart?"

"Pretty good."

Jaret gave him a playful punch on the arm. "You ready to do some partying?"

Amanda gave him a little scowl.

"What do you think I've been doing? You've got some catching up to do, son."

Jon came over and took Jaret away to his "office" leaving Steve and Amanda alone. She studied him, concern showing in her eyes. "Heather still out on the boat?"

Steve nodded. "I've accepted the fact that she loves her whales more than me. I can handle it." He winked.

Seemingly out of nowhere she said, "Watch yourself on that motorcycle."

"Don't worry, I'm fine."

She nodded in the direction Jaret had gone. "Living with one problem child is bad enough. I don't need to worry about two of you."

Jaret came back and sat with Amanda. His eyes seemed to bulge out of his head. Jon offered them drinks. Jaret had a screwdriver and Amanda had a wine cooler. Steve had his old standby Jack Daniels on the rocks. They sat together drinking and chatting for awhile. Jaret and Steve smoked weed and took occasional trips to the office with Jon while Amanda visited with some of the girls.

Steve found himself alone again, eyes closed, listening to the music when the Rolling Stones *Sympathy for the Devil* blasted into the room stirring a flurry of thoughts and images.

The flicker of candlelight through drawn curtains.

The altar with the big gold pentagram with the inverted crucifix.

Carla's "friends" naked and paired off in male-female pairs and the low murmur of chants droning, "Say-tan. Say-tan."

Carla nude on the altar with a young dark-skinned man wearing a hooded black stole mounting her.

Another man reading from a battered leather-bound book.

*"In nomine Patris et Filii et Spiritus Sancti et domini nostri Satanas."*

Their immediacy made Steve feel claustrophobic and he couldn't breathe, so he bolted to his feet, needing to get out of there.

Amanda spotted him heading for the door and followed him out with Jaret in tow.

The moon shone full and clear as if calling him. "You sure you can drive?" Amanda asked catching up to him and putting her hand on his arm.

"No problem. I'm good." He put on his helmet.

"You sure?"

The look she gave him made him uneasy.

"Don't worry."

"You sure you can handle all that machine?" Jaret said, half in jest and half in concern.

Steve started the bike, revved the engine a couple of times, and rocketed out into the street. The momentum forced him to lean hard to make the turn and as he dipped his rear tire lost traction in some gravel and he went down sliding into the other side of the street. He looked up just in time to see a van bearing down on him followed by a blinding flash of light.

# DEATH

# CHAPTER TEN

Darkness.

Numb and disoriented, Steve opened his eyes.

Several people crowded around a van. He craned his neck to see what was going on but they blocked his view. He reached out to tap someone on the shoulder and jerked his hand back, shocked when his finger went *through* them.

He examined his hand and gasped when he saw through it, then he looked down. His body had the same translucent quality. Without thinking he walked through the bodies of the people in the crowd as if *they* were ethereal, stopping dead when he made it to the front of the crowd.

A motorcycle identical to his Harley lay crushed beneath the van, a mangled body twisted within the wreckage. He stumbled around to the other side of the wreck and stared at it. One glazed eye glared back at him and the other dangled halfway down its cheek. His knees gave way and he sagged as darkness claimed him once again. He struggled to rationalize it all as a dream, but its surrealistic quality heightened its vividness, and with this hyper-lucidity the answer became clear.

*I'm dead!*

The sight of his blood-soaked mutilated body stunned him, but the full blow hit when he turned and saw the ashen faces of Jon, Jaret, and Amanda frozen in horrified grimaces. He ran to them screaming, but no one acknowledged him. Amanda buried her head in Jaret's shoulder and sobbed, while Jaret and Jon looked on, helpless. Overcome with emotion, Steve tried to speak again, but all that came out were unintelligible sounds and his despair turned from anger to frustration, followed by hopelessness. He couldn't remember ever feeling such anguish.

As if mocking his suffering, his emotional turmoil had no physical sensations. He cried without tears, feared without chills or dryness of throat and felt nothing on his skin except a muted sense of touch as if a giant glove encased his whole body. The textures and temperatures of normal sensations had gone.

He felt the pull of gravity holding him down, but he had no sense of weight and his perceptions went no further than his emotions. As his initial shock faded the full weight of what happened enveloped him like an unwelcome fog rolling in off the ocean bringing with it a gauzy sense of separation from the people he loved, particularly Heather. His longing for her filled him with an acute sense of loss as though some vital part of his anatomy had been torn out.

An ambulance came and he stared in silence as paramedics extricated his battered body from the wreckage and put a sheet over it.

He watched the ambulance drive off, taking his lifeless, disfigured body with it.

*I can't believe it. Am I really dead?*

He looked down at himself again, clapped his hands together and stared at them. No sound and no physical sensations. Nothing but frustrating emotions with no outlet to express them. He kneeled and punched at the ground. His hand sank in up to his elbow as if he had punched at air. *There has to be more than this.*

The crowd dispersed and an unseen force pulled him to Jaret and Amanda. He struggled against it, but it was beyond his control so he gave in and followed them to their car as if led by an invisible leash. He stopped next to the back door, afraid of what would happen if they drove away. When he reached for the door handle his hand came out the other side through the window. He pulled it back and did it again watching it pass unhindered, then the car pulled away drawing him with it. He slid into the back seat through the closed door aware that he existed in a world of forms that he could move through with little sense of physical interaction, as if encased in a giant, insulating glove.

Amanda's sobs filled the car. Even though they had no awareness of him, Steve shared their grief. When they got home Amanda spoke for the first time since the accident.

"I know this sounds weird," she said amidst her sobs, "but I feel like Steve is here with us right now."

Jaret hugged her tight. Steve wished he could say something to comfort them, but knew it would be in vain.

Two days passed with neither of them barely speaking while going through the motions of life like *they* were the walking dead. Steve felt trapped between them like the victim of some cruel cosmic joke that forced him to bear witness to their grief, rubbing his face in it, drawn stronger to whoever had the deepest sorrow in each passing moment until the phone rang on the third day.

*Heather*, Steve thought. *I know it.* He dreaded the inevitable.

"Hello," Jaret said in a subdued tone.

"Jaret!" Heather said, "I've got a horrible feeling something's happened to Steve. I've been trying to call him. Have you heard anything from him?"

Jaret remained silent and Steve felt his struggle.

"Jaret, are you okay?" Heather asked.

Steve heard the rising panic in her voice.

"What's happening?" She cried.

"Heather," Jaret managed, "I need to come over and talk to you."

"What's wrong?"

"I'll be right over."

"Tell me now! What's wrong?"

"I don't know how to tell you..."

"Tell me what?" She asked, frantic.

"Steve's dead."

In the silence that followed Steve flashed to Heather's side.

"What?"

"He died in a motorcycle accident."

Heather dropped the phone and crumpled to the floor in a flood of tears, her body convulsing in sobs.

Steve looked on, helpless.

"Heather... I'm sorry," he said. He wept in his heart and his mind spun, but no tears came, his "body" unable to express emotion. He wrapped his arms around her to comfort her and they went through her. He heard Jaret's voice through the dropped cell phone.

"Heather! Heather! You alright?"

She reached for the phone. "Yes," she answered between sobs.

"We'll come over and keep you company..."

"No," she cut in. "I need to be alone."

"You sure?"

Her voice quavered. "I'll call if I need anything."

She hit the END button, dropped the phone again, and curled up into a fetal position. When darkness fell she went sobbing to her room and lay down on her bed with her head in her arms. Steve sat on the edge of the bed beside her, numb with unexpressed emotion.

"Oh Steve," Heather sobbed, "If you can hear me, may God be with you."

He wanted to let her know he heard her, but knew she couldn't hear him.

In the next instant he found himself at his parent's house where his father held his mother while she wept on his shoulder. When his father called his sister and told her what had happened, Steve materialized at her house and as each person was informed of his death the force of their emotions pulled him to them, leaving him no choice but to bear witness to their grief. He often experienced the uncanny sensation of being in two or more places simultaneously, fully aware of all of them.

For the next week he felt helplessly drawn to whoever experienced the most intense grief. Mick was one of the last people to find out. He took the news quietly, then called Smokey at the karate studio and informed him. That night in class when everyone lined up, Smokey broke the news.

"Some of you may have already heard," he said solemnly, "but for those of you who haven't, Steve, one of our brothers was killed in a motorcycle accident. Let's share a moment of silence and meditate on the thought of him and join our thoughts in a send off with some positive energy to wherever he may be."

Steve felt himself charge with a rejuvenating energy. His experiences since dying had all been negative, draining, and chaotic. This was his first positive moment since dying.

He watched his body being cremated after a small ceremony attended by his immediate family and when it was gone he felt as if his distance from the world had doubled. He felt lighter in what he could only define as airy and ethereal, but his mood felt darker, his essence abandoned in ways he couldn't comprehend.

After his family separated he once more became subject to being pulled from one person to the next according to who had the most sadness. He spent most of his time around Heather with Amanda being a close second. He never realized how much they had really cared for him.

As time wore on the pull from people subsided and he started gaining temporary control over where he was. Sometimes he was irresistibly drawn to somebody, but with less frequency. During his free moments he discovered that he could transport himself at will to wherever he wanted to go in an instant, much like he had in dreams.

As more time elapsed he sensed when someone thought about him by the way they popped into his head, but he had grown strong enough to choose whether to go to them or not until he became aware of a familiar presence that he felt, but could not fully perceive. At the moment he felt like he gained full command over his actions the mysterious presence revealed itself.

# CHAPTER ELEVEN

Steve sat talking to Heather one night as she slept knowing she couldn't hear him, but talking nonetheless, trying to find comfort in his own words. His whole existence had grown more dreamlike and he wished he could slip through the invisible barrier that separated them and go into her dreams to be with her.

"Heather, if only you could hear me. It's agonizing to be so close without being able to touch or talk to you from the other side of a wall I can't see." He held his hand in front of his face studying it's translucence. "My stupidity has alienated me from you and everyone else. My own unhappiness is bad enough, but watching you suffer and knowing I'm responsible is worse – and the loneliness – I can't take it, but I can't end it."

He covered his face with his hands and fell silent until a distinct feeling of being watched stole over him like before with Heather when he was alive, only now it had no negativity. Instead it felt inviting, as though it offered an antidote to his loneliness and sense of exile. It continued to grow behind him until he couldn't deny it. Wheeling around he found himself face to face with Carla and his world came to a halt in a puzzling freeze frame that held him suspended in emptiness.

She smiled and he saw the wounded look in her eyes, then his surroundings blurred until they floated together in timeless empty space being everywhere and nowhere at the same time.

"How are you Steve? I've missed you."

The sight of her filled him with apprehension, but his stark isolation and need for companionship overrode it. He stumbled toward her dazed and full of anguish, embracing her, overjoyed to discover that she felt solid, but different. Insulated – without warmth.

"I've been waiting for you," she said softly.

She looked just as he remembered her, only her body had the same translucent quality as his. His shock faded, replaced by a giddy mixture of fear and happiness from somewhere within him, a muted shadow, devoid of sensation and emotion like a memory that lived more in his head than in his heart.

A rush of scenes from the last night he saw her flitted through his mind filling him with doubt, each image flashing like a silent warning klaxon, the altar, the gold pentagram with the inverted cross, the chanting, Carla nude on the altar…

His remembered love and loneliness pushed the imagery from his mind.

"Carla," he whispered, searching her eyes. "I didn't think I'd ever see you again. I thought about you a lot, especially in my dreams."

"I spent a lot of time around you. That's why you thought about me so much."

Their surroundings fluttered and strobed into focus until they stood on a seashore. She took him by the hand and started walking. Unlike his contact with her he thought it strange not to feel the wind or smell the salt air.

"Why did you wait so long before talking to me?" he asked.

"I had to wait until your will grew strong enough to free itself from the emotions of your family and friends. Your soul was at the mercy of their feelings which you were obligated to struggle with until you gained your own power. Their love for you drew you to them and their emotions held your soul until the sadness of your death diminished and your will emerged stronger than their emotion. From what I've learned it's the process of rebirth into this new reality. The same process that a hatchling goes through to break free from its egg or a plant breaking free from the shell of its seed to embrace the light of the sun."

"You've been watching all this time?"

Steve slowed his pace, but Carla pulled him along. "I gradually made my presence known to you. I didn't want to shock you and I couldn't contact you until you extricated yourself from your lower dimensional attachments. We are all subject to the forces of cosmic law beyond our comprehension and have no choice but to abide by them. You had to complete the rebirth part of your transition into this higher dimension on your own. I've been sent as a spiritual midwife and helpmate for you."

Steve pulled his hand away from her and stopped.

"Cosmic law, rebirth, and higher dimensions?"

Carla smiled wistfully and spoke as if explaining the obvious to a to a child. "We now live in the ethereal realms and travel in higher vibrational astral bodies which can move about freely from place to place."

"Like in dreams."

She nodded. "Exactly!"

He held his hands out wide. "So how do I know that this isn't all a dream?" Scenes from the last time he had seen Carla alive flashed through him again followed by images of his own horrific death and his intoxicated state of mind that preceded it. He shook his head. "We didn't exactly leave our lives behind in a higher state of consciousness."

She opened her mouth to respond and the words flew from him before she could speak.

"No disrespect intended, but who the fuck sent you as my guide into this higher dimension? The last time I saw you, you were getting fucked in a satanic mass." He regretted saying it when she lowered her head with a saddened expression, but something inside him lightened when he got it out.

When she didn't answer and the silence between them grew awkward he asked again. "Who sent you as my help mate?"

"The ascended masters," she said breathlessly. "Our teachers and guides. They say it's important for you to be brought through the transition with someone close to you." She looked up, her expression brightening. "You and I are destined to be one spirit." She took both his hands in hers and looked into his eyes, searching. "Twin flames."

"Ascended masters? And who are they?"

"Bodhisattvas!"

"Like in the Steely Dan song?"

"Yes."

"And what is a bodhisattva?"

She went into schoolmarm mode again. "Someone who is able to reach nirvana but delays it out of compassion to save suffering people. The first part comes from budh which means awaken and evolved into bodhi which means perfect knowledge. The last part sattva means being and essence. Together they mean a person whose essence is perfect.

They guide us in an intelligent order that rules the cosmos and we're subject to it whether living, or so-called dead."

The dark imagery returned and Steve shook his head to try and make it go away. "Sorry, but I don't buy it. What kind of perfect beings condone devil worship, group fucking, skulls, pentagrams, upside down crosses and all that other sick shit?"

"Ones with compassion," she said, sounding indignant. "Ones who plumb the darkness for lost souls and save them from the hellish abyss they are being sucked into."

Her words stopped the torrent of dark thoughts.

"Why?," he said, filling the emptiness. "Why reach out and save someone who worships hell and the devil?"

She leaned in close and in a soft wavering childlike treble said, "Forgiveness."

"Are you saying that's what happened to you?"

"Forgiveness," she said again, her eyes imploring, "which brings the gift of compassion. They rescued me in my darkest moment of torment and saved me from the evil that possessed me."

Possessed? He wanted to argue more, but the words wouldn't come.

"Forgiveness," she said breathlessly. "I had no control over what I said or did. They had taken over my life and made me their slave. I was helpless..." She stared at the ground.

After an extended silence she started walking, gently pulling him along. Everything she said overwhelmed and confused him and he didn't know what to say or think, so he didn't resist. Forgiveness?

"Now that we're disembodied," she said leaning in close, "we need to go through a period of retraining so we can reincarnate back on the physical plane and live complete lives to follow in the footsteps of the masters and become like them, then we will be able to guide others."

"How do we do that?"

"Mortals on the physical plane give us opportunities to use their bodies so we can experience sensations through them with our higher sense of awareness." She smiled "This allows us to learn more and satisfy our desires."

As amazing as it all sounded he couldn't wrap his mind around it. "They let us use their bodies?"

"It's more accurate to say that they present us with opportunities."

"But..."

"It's a higher level agreement we all make in spirit before entering the earth plane."

"I don't like the sound of it."

"It's going to take some time for you to adjust." She squeezed his arm, reassuring him. "You'll understand more after you learn some techniques." Her eyes brightened. "You've already learned one on your own."

"Which one is that?"

"Freeing yourself from the influence of people's emotions. Instead of going to them like you used to, they pop into your head when they think about you. You have the choice of joining them or not. This can be used to your advantage."

"How?"

"It creates an opening and a connection."

Steve slowed the conflicting thoughts tumbling through his mind and listened to the waves crashing on the beach and the far away cry of a gull, puzzling over his lack of physically feeling emotions and sensations. Seeing and hearing were all he knew and even they felt muted in an inexplicable way that he couldn't grasp, just like he couldn't grasp what she was telling him.

"Bodhisattvas have dedicated themselves to shaping our destiny by training us in the arts of physical awareness and one important facet of embracing that fully is sensory immersion. Once we learn to master those skills in these forms we can reincarnate in mortal bodies and refine our awareness, including our god-given desires. Our destiny is to live full and complete lives."

"It sounds awesome, but I have to be honest with you. It strikes me as too good to be true."

"I know how you feel." She pushed her silky black hair back from her face. Though he saw the effects of the wind shaking leaves on trees, Carla's hair didn't move in the breeze and Steve couldn't help but notice the muted radiance of her skin. It looked beautiful in its own unique way in spite of its weird translucence. Beautiful in what he thought of as a bubble of stillness, like an otherworldly work of moving art. "I felt the same way, she continued, but now..."

"I don't think I'm ready. I need some time to think this through."

"You're still recovering from the shock of losing your physical body. Once you've adjusted, everything will fall into place."

"It's just that – To be honest the idea scares me."

She shook her head. "You'll see what I mean when you perform your own actions through a mortal enhanced by your higher awareness. It starts out slow, but as you become more proficient your opportunities increase."

Steve stopped walking again. "I don't mean to sound like a stick in the mud, but it sounds like we'll be manipulating them without their consent."

She shook her head again. "Like I said, they give up control of their bodies. It's a pre-arranged sharing agreement made in spirit before entering the earth plane. All we do is step in and take over. They don't even realize it's happening and end up thinking it's their own thoughts and actions, and they don't remember anything when it's over. It works as a form of protection so they're not influenced by what *we* do."

Carla cocked her head to one side as if listening for something. They stopped by a clump of rocks and she tilted her head again.

"Do you understand what I told you about waiting until your will was strong enough to overcome the force of other people's emotions?"

"Yeah."

"We move ourselves around here by willing it. All you have to do is will yourself to be in the presence of the masters and you and I will go there together."

"Now?"

"They're waiting. Close your eyes and do what I've told you."

Steve closed his eyes and concentrated, sensing a change in his surroundings. When he opened them he stood next to Carla in front of a long table. Thirteen shimmering angelic figures wearing white robes that radiated a light so bright, Steve could barely keep his eyes on them sat behind it. Part of him recoiled as he felt them probing him with even brighter stares that he could not bear for more than the briefest of glimpses.

"We're happy you made it," the central figure said in a low tone that resonated both inside and outside of Steve. "I trust Carla is guiding you through your rebirthing comfortably."

"She is," Steve answered, his voice barely audible.

"As Carla has told you, we are the Lords overseeing planet Earth, appointed by the most high to watch over the affairs of mortals. It is our duty to supervise the retraining of souls so you can go back and take your rightful place in the third dimension with total awareness. It is the will of the most high and our wish that you find your training enlightening and we are confident that you will serve us well."

Serve us? Steve cringed from the intensity of it all so he bowed his head and nodded. Questions brimmed in his mind, but he didn't dare ask. The masters faded and he stood with Carla in the middle of a spacious green meadow, relieved to be in a "normal" setting again, whatever that was.

Groups of people gathered in circles with one person who glimmered a little more than the others leading each group. When Steve felt comfortable there the scenery changed to a forest where more classes were being taught in a similar fashion.

He marveled at the changes as they passed from one tranquil scene to the next through every scene imaginable from mountains to seashores. At each place everybody looked content and everything transpired in a state of blissful perfection.

# CHAPTER TWELVE

Steve's perceptions blurred and his surroundings shifted into a meadow like the one they had been to earlier. A gentle breeze rustled the leaves on the trees and Steve was once again struck by the odd sensation of seeing and hearing with only those two senses while his senses of smell, taste, and touch remained muted along with his visceral sense of emotion. It dawned on him that he felt no hunger or any desire for food which contributed to his sense of emptiness.

A slender man dressed in white with long curly flaxen hair and corn flower blue eyes came forward. "Pleased to meet you," he said in a welcoming tone. "I'm Elijah."

"Nice to meet you," Steve took his extended hand, feeling a firm handshake.

"Come, meet the rest of the group." Elijah guided him over to a group of four sitting in a circle on the grass.

Michelle, a cute, brown-haired all American looking girl with long hair, bangs and brown eyes that matched her hair sat beside Rob, a balding bearded man with dark hair and a stocky build. Lisa, a shy, hazel-eyed plump red head, and Mike, a short muscular man with bristly brown hair in a close cropped crew cut and tatted arms sat across from Rob and Michelle. Carla and Steve completed the group of six with Elijah leading them, making seven.

Everyone was new to the group and teaching, so Elijah gave them a little time get acquainted before getting their attention.

"I'm going to be guiding you through your training", he said, eyeing each member of the group individually. "This first part deals with dreaming and vibrations which I think you will enjoy, but first I want to lay down some basics, so please bear with me."

His expression changed from light and open to a look of concentration and his eyes brightened. "As you have all been discovering, our bodies vibrate at different frequencies. Physical bodies move slower because they vibrate at lower frequencies making it easy for us to perceive them."

He put his hand on his chest. "We, on the other hand, move at a higher vibration so they can't perceive us." He smiled showing a perfect set of teeth "But we can perceive ourselves and them too."

He looked at each member of the group again one at a time to make his point. Michelle nodded emphatically, Rob winked, Lisa put her hands together in a prayer-like fashion, and Mike gave a curt nod. Carla took Steve's hand and gave it a light squeeze.

"We can cultivate the ability to change our vibration to match theirs," Elijah continued," in essence tuning in to them in what is called resonance, the same concept that allows radios to match the stations transmitting frequencies." He gave them a broad grin. "In this case you will be the transmitter and your subjects will be the receivers, then it's a simple matter for us to slip into their bodies and experience the third dimension through them. In the beginning you have to match up what you want to experience with a person predisposed to that type of behavior but as you learn to master this skill, you'll gain more freedom."

Elijah's eyes rested on Steve as if addressing him directly. Their conviction added to the conviction in his voice. "As you experience things through different people your perceptions will be colored by each one's individual temperament. Since everyone is different each sensation will be individual and unique, varying in depth and intensity from person to person. There are some you won't be able to work with which are considered exceptions to the rule. You'll know when you come across one. Not only will you be able to see them, but they will give you a definitive sense of warning. Stay clear of them. Any attempt to interact with them will result in consequences you don't want to experience." He held up a finger. "Trust me on that!"

"What kind of consequences?" Steve asked.

The rest of the group looked at him like he had done something wrong by asking the question.

Elijah held up a hand. "Let's take a little field trip to give you a demonstration."

Steve's surroundings melted away and realigned with the rest of the group as they came into focus in a city park.

"We're in Balboa Park in San Diego," Elijah said. "Pay close attention. We're going to observe mortals in their everyday life to gain insight into resonance and dreaming."

He paced back and forth as he spoke, gesturing with his hands when he wanted to make a point. "The first thing I want to demonstrate is the energy fields that are referred to as auras. By learning how to read and interpret them we can get a feel for how to resonate with them and what type of manipulation can most easily be performed." He paused and scanned the group to let his words sink in before continuing.

"People with like temperaments have similar auras, though no two are exactly the same. You can judge a person's moods and how easy it will be to work with them by observing the color and intensity of their aura, and as you gain proficiency in interpreting these indicators you will learn how to motivate them through directed resonance."

Elijah squatted before the group and narrowed his eyes as he spoke. "The proper method of perceiving an aura is to close your eyes halfway until you observe your subject through the hairs on your eyelids while concentrating on the area around their head, then gently direct your will toward them."

He squinted toward each member of the group to demonstrate and had each person try it on their own, then he gestured toward different people in the park. Steve chose a man who looked to be in his mid-thirties with short brown hair dressed in a light blue shirt and a dark tie sitting on a park bench. Studying him through half closed eyelids, he tried his best to imitate Elijah's example. He struggled for a few moments until a lime green colored light with small steaks of red popped into his perception, surrounding the man's head like the flame of a candle. An attractive long-legged blonded girl walked by and the red streaks grew wider and brighter.

Elijah encouraged everyone to try different subjects, so Steve next chose a tastefully dressed middle aged woman who gave him the impression of being snobbish. Her aura blazed red with streaks of violet while talking to an older woman with the same disposition whose aura flickered yellow with a large streak of red. Their auras wavered as they gestured in a heated discussion. As each of them grew excited in turn the red part of their auras flared. The older woman's didn't look as intense as the younger woman's and neither looked as intense as the young man's.

Children played off to his left with their auras blazing like rainbows with no particular hue showing stronger than the rest. He looked over and saw other members of the group squinting in their own ways while watching their own subjects. Elijah called their attention to an older couple strolling up the path together. Her aura had a uniform violet hue and his shone solid blue. Both radiated intensely.

"People of this type are perfect examples of the exceptions to the rule that you've been warned about." Elijah nodded slowly and his voice betrayed a hint of uneasiness. "They should be avoided at all costs." He focused his attention on Steve.

"I don't see anything wrong," Steve said. "They look happy to me." He felt attracted to them as they walked by. "In fact I feel connected to them somehow..."

Elijah held up a finger. "Excellent observation Steve," then to the group, "What Steve has so astutely pointed out is the attraction of seduction which is the essence of evil. That sense of being pulled in is the warning that I told you about. Do you feel it?"

Everyone nodded.

With a curt nod, Elijah became his authoritative self again. "All the colors you observe are indicators of different moods and personality types," he continued. "Anytime you see red it's an opportunity for you to act. Its intensity is important too. It's a direct indicator of their life force. In fact if you see someone close to death they will have no aura at all."

"Wow!" Lisa said in a hushed whisper.

"Low intensity auras are not good to work with because of the ebbing life force, except when the subject is sleeping. We'll discuss that later. Right now I want to give you guidelines to go by when dealing with colors."

He sat down on the grass and leaned toward the group lowering his voice in a conspiratorial manner. "As I pointed out, blue, purple, or any single color auras, with the exception of red, are dangerous and should be avoided. Multicolored auras are the best because they can be influenced easily. The idea is to bring out as much red as possible. As you've seen, children have the greatest variety of colors and many older people tend to have lots of red. They are both easy marks and not considered to be much of a challenge, but they have their uses."

He turned and pointed to the girl watcher sitting on the bench. "That young man is an excellent subject. Because of his age his life force is in its healthiest state of flux. The greater the strength of an aura, the greater the intensity of your experience through that person, but a healthy energy field also poses greater challenges." Elijah inclined his head toward the bench. "He's a perfect subject to experience dreaming with. Let's follow him back to his apartment."

After a series of flickers the class crowded around the man's bed that night.

"When he goes to sleep you'll notice his aura decreasing. When it reaches a certain point he'll ease into a dreaming state which we'll enter into with him as observers. His will is going to be the guiding force throughout the experience and it won't be focused, so we will be witnessing a disjointed state of dreaming. Eventually you will have opportunities to participate in other's dreams, but for now I want you to focus on learning the proper method of entering."

The group watched in silence as the man drifted to sleep and his aura diminished to a fraction of its normal size.

"The next facet of our instruction deals with what we call the dream gaze." Elijah said. "The same method used for observing auras with one exception." He shook his finger. "You need to direct your will at the point in the middle of your subject's forehead, directly between, but slightly above the eyes."

Elijah stood beside the young man and pointed to the spot, demonstrating his technique and directing the group to focus their wills together. Steve felt himself become lighter while shrinking toward the man. The rest of the group appeared to turn to smoke and float toward the young man's head along with him, immersing in a scene, witnessing its events, feeling part of them, yet somehow removed.

They stood on a hill overlooking a field watching a medieval battle where their subject was surrounded by attackers while fighting for his life. Despite the odds he overcame his opponents and made his way to a horse that he rode toward a large castle that loomed on the horizon.

When he reached it he jumped off and walked across a drawbridge over an alligator infested moat and fought his way through a maze of tunnels full of warriors until he came to the top of a tower where a beautiful girl was tied to a rack. Wielding his sword like an axe he cut through the ropes and took her into his arms, kissing her passionately, then turned to see a sword flying toward his head. Light glinted off it and it turned into a meteor that missed his spaceship by inches. Manipulating the controls, he positioned the ship to reenter the atmosphere, but something went wrong and it disintegrated, so he flew back to earth under his own power, circled it a few times and landed back in his bedroom where he settled back into a dreamless sleep.

The group materialized in the same places they had been when they started, all of them expressing individual looks of awe from what they witnessed. Elijah whisked them back to the meadows and after a lengthy discussion he gave everyone an assignment.

"I want all of you to go visit some of your mortal friends and see if you can get into their dreams. They'll be easier for you to work with because their thoughts of you will still be fresh in their minds. If you will it, you might be able to take an active part in their dreams, but don't be disappointed if you can't. That will come in it's own time. I want to stress that our subject's dream was chaotic because we made no attempts to influence it. I want all of you to try and make your friend's dreams valid by utilizing what you've been taught and experimenting on your own. If you come across any solid auras, get the hell out of there. You'll all know when and where to meet again and when we do we'll share our experiences and see what we can learn from each other."

# CHAPTER THIRTEEN

Torn between the conflicting worlds and memories of Heather and Carla, Steve materialized in Heather's room where she sat up in bed reading Elizabeth Kübler Ross's *On Death and Dying*. He sat at her side until she put the book down and turned off the light, then he studied her with a deep seated, subdued sense of longing that had no physical sensation connected with it.

When her greenish-orange aura dimmed to a soft radiance, he focused his dream gaze on her and became lighter as if evaporating, then compressed while being drawn toward her like smoke sucked into a fan until he appeared in her kitchen which felt the same to him whether in a dream or out. Heather stood with her back to him, cooking something at the stove, unaware of his presence.

He didn't want to scare her, but he wanted to see if he could influence what happened so he closed his eyes and thought about it. When he opened them she turned and spotted him.

"Steve!" A dish fell from her hands. "This can't be. You're dead!"

"Never mind that," he answered, "I'm here now. That's all that matters."

She stared at him wide-eyed, then sounding despondent said, "It's a dream."

He took her by the arm and to his disappointment she had the same sterile feeling as Carla.

"Heather, yes, it's a dream, but at least we can talk which is more than we could do before. Come on." He willed them to a spot on a cliff by the ocean which came easily. Having control over their actions and environment gave him some comfort, but it was nothing like he remembered. Without the feel of the wind and the scent of salt air it felt lackluster.

Tears streamed down her cheeks. "I've missed you so much," she whispered.

He absentmindedly wiped them from her face, but felt no wetness.

"I've missed you too." He cried without tears and took her by the hands. Looking into her eyes he saw that they were just as he remembered them, only now they held recognition, something he hadn't seen since passing over.

In spite of the deadness of his experience Steve wanted to stay with her, but without knowing how or why he knew his time was up. He grabbed and held her tight, but his surroundings evaporated and he shrank, expanding again at the end of her bed, watching her stir before sitting up in bed, tears streaming down her cheeks, her eyes red and swollen.

She covered her face with her hands. "Don't leave me!"

He watched her while sterile emotional hell took root. "Oh Heather," he whispered. "I'm so sorry I put you through this."

"It was only a dream," she sobbed.

"Fuck!" He kicked at her nightstand and lost his balance when his foot went through it and felt nothing when he hit the floor.

Heather laid back down and cried herself to sleep.

I'm never going to do that with her again, he thought. I can't take the pain of watching her.

He wandered out of her house and walked aimlessly through the neighborhood thinking he might have better luck with Jaret and Amanda. Maybe if he asserted his will more he could gain control of the whole dream, and maybe there wouldn't be as much emotional attachment.

He went to their house and entered easily into Jaret's dream. "Hey, Steve," Jaret said from his couch as if nothing out of the ordinary had happened. "It's great to see you big guy. How're you doing?"

"I've been okay. How about you guys?"

"We're doing fine," Amanda answered surprising him when she came in from the kitchen, "but we've missed you."

Her unexpected appearance prompted Steve with an impulse he couldn't deny, so he willed himself out of Jaret's dream and reentered Amanda's, back into the same scene he had just left.

"How are things going at work, Jaret?"

"You know. Same ol, same ol."

"You guys getting along without me?"

"Sure."

Steve willed himself out of Amanda's dream and went back in again through Jaret, disbelieving that they had shared the same dream.

"Steve," Amanda said softly. "How come you left like you did?"

"I came right back."

No, I mean the night you died."

"I..." he stammered. "I couldn't help myself."

"It's been rough on us."

Her words hit him with a tangible, but invisible slap.

"I have to go."

He faded out and returned the next morning in a state of confusion hoping they'd talk about their dream, but they didn't. Instead they sat around barely talking, each of them lost in their thoughts.

I'm not going to experiment with them or Heather anymore, Steve thought. All it accomplishes is the reopening of wounds that haven't even healed yet. I'm not going to try with anyone...

Mick! All of that stuff he talked about doing in the jungle with those plants he called the flesh of the gods. Maybe my experience with him will be different. Maybe I can get into his dreams and he can explain things. He always seemed to know what was going on with me when I was alive.

He found Mick fast asleep. When he focused his gaze the sight of Mick's aura jolted him. Not only was it solid, it shone a brilliant sky blue with a flawless intensity Steve didn't think possible. It's otherworldly beauty radiated unlike anything he had seen and he felt drawn to it with a force he had never experienced before. He stared at it overwhelmed by its power, torn between rising fear and fascination.

A fluctuating multicolored lattice of complex shifting geometric patterns appeared surrounding Mick like an energetic cage of some kind. Though Mick's aura drew him powerfully, the closer he got to the energy lattice the brighter it radiated and the more disoriented he became to the point of panic.

Flesh of the gods, he told himself, followed by the thought of Pandora's Box and demons. Fuck that!

In the next moment he popped into the group shaken to the core of his being. Elijah greeted him with a startled look, but said nothing.

One by one Michelle, Rob, Lisa, Mike, and Carla described their experiences which were all similar to the first group fantasy dream they had shared with the young girl watcher.

"Well Steve." Elijah eyed him thoughtfully. "We've heard from everyone but you. Am I right in assuming that your experience was different?"

"How did you know?"

Elijah answered with a cryptic smile. "I can sense these things. What happened?"

"I looked up an old girlfriend." He glanced sideways at Carla who scowled. "But it was depressing and I thought about quitting when I got the idea to look up some other old friends. That's when things got interesting."

He stopped to gather his thoughts and saw Carla's displeasure fading. The group leaned in giving him their full attention, especially Elijah.

"The dream was nothing spectacular until I discovered that three of us were dreaming the same dream. I was able to leave one person's dream and go back into that same dream through the other person.

Lisa went wide-eyed and put her hand to her mouth and Michelle looked shocked while Mike looked confused and Rob frowned.

"Seriously?" Carla said.

"I went in and out of the same dream through two different people three times."

"Quite an accomplishment," Elijah said solemnly. "It's rare, even among experienced practitioners." He raised his eyebrows.

"But that's not the biggest thing you came across, is it?"

"I went to look up one more old friend and he turned out to have a solid aura, but it was even weirder and scarier than that!"

Everyone looked at him with mixed expressions of fear, apprehension, and confusion.

"He was covered by what looked like a cage of energy made of different colored complicated geometry patterns that glowed and changed. The closer I got the stronger and more complicated they got. I thought the intense beauty of his aura was going to swallow me, but the closer I got to the energy patterns the brighter they glowed and the faster they moved. "It really tripped me out!"

Everyone looked to Elijah, who put his hands together and bowed his head. "Black magic," he said under his breath, then louder. "A trap put there by a sorcerer called an arkana, but not from the Latin root word that means hidden or secret, although there is an aspect of that, but from the South American Quechua root spelled with a K that means to block or bar. From what you described, this was a very sophisticated trap that draws you like the proverbial moth to the flame only this one would snap shut like a bear trap." He clapped his hands together to make the point.

"There is no known means of escape."

# CHAPTER FOURTEEN

Carla and Steve sat together in the midday desert oblivious to the searing temperatures. No wind could be seen and silence enveloped them.

"So tell me," Carla said, leaning in close. "How did you manage to go into your friend's dreams and direct their wills so that all three of you experienced the same dream? According to Elijah beginners can't do that. What's your secret?"

"There's no secret. It was easy and it felt natural."

"Really?" She seemed lost in thought, then, "Let's go find Elijah," she said like an excited little girl. "I can't wait to see what he's going to teach us next."

"Okay", he said, letting her excitement rub off on him. "I just now got an urge to go find him myself."

She took him by the hand and they closed their eyes, concentrating. Steve jumped when he opened them. They hadn't gone anywhere. Elijah and the rest of their group appeared before them. Everyone laughed at his surprise, including Carla.

"We decided to join *you*," Elijah said amidst the laughter. "I hope we're not intruding."

Steve shrugged and found himself grinning in spite of himself. "Not at all. You just caught me off guard. I didn't expect to see everyone here."

When their mirth subsided Elijah addressed the group. "Today we're going to talk about advanced dreaming techniques and the assertion of your will on mortal subjects, two areas that are interrelated.

By using them together you'll learn to influence mortal experience in a subtler manner which is one of the first steps toward re-experiencing three dimensional reality through a living being."

He put his hands together as if praying and a distant look came to his eyes. "In the beginning you'll only be able to affect their thought flow. If you're lucky you might see a physical act. If you do, it will give you an indication of how much influence you've exerted. Don't expect too much at this stage of the game, unless you're Steve."

He looked at Steve and winked. "I want each of you to pick a mortal friend to work with. Someone of the same sex, preferably in a similar situation that you were in before you passed over."

"Why do they have to be like us?" Mike asked.

"The reason will become apparent. It's important to put some thought behind your choice. Pick someone you feel will be easy to work with in the future. The more you're able to interact with them now, the easier it will be later."

He paced back and forth as he talked with his hands clasped behind his back. "The reason I want you to pick a friend like I've described is because you'll already have some affinity with their thoughts. It should be easier for you to influence them on a subtle level like in dreaming. You can build on that until your friend begins identifying with *your* thoughts. When that happens they'll think your thoughts are theirs which will make it easier for you to manifest yourself through them and embrace dense physical reality again."

"That makes sense," Carla said.

"Resonance," Rob added.

Elijah smiled and nodded. "I want each of you to find a suitable subject and stay with them. I'll come advise you on your choice."

Steve didn't like the idea of someone thinking his thoughts were theirs. He had bad memories about that happening to him, but he couldn't remember when. I need more time to sort this out, he thought. Who am I going to pick? Everyone I went to last time left me feeling like shit and I don't feel right screwing with their thoughts and emotions.

He exchanged glances with Carla who smiled before fading out.

Without knowing who or how to pick, Steve went to Mick's power spot in the mountains to try and figure things out, but when he tried to narrow them down to specifics his mind went blank. He puzzled over his conflicting feelings between Heather and Carla thinking he had been spending too much time with Carla while avoiding Heather because he didn't want to bring her any more sadness, but he still felt drawn to her.

He surveyed the valley below feeling the same loneliness he had while alive, like something was missing. Thankfully he hadn't blacked out, but he sensed lapses – like his thoughts had not been entirely his own.

Elijah's going to come looking for me sooner or later wondering why I haven't done anything and I have no idea who to pick for a subject. He stared up at the sky as if he could find the answer there, then it hit.

Mick!

Fear and excitement filled him and he flew into a series of conflicting deliberations.

No way. He has a solid aura.

He's my friend. I can trust him.

He looked around remembering their shared time at the spot he now sat in and his fear gave way to curiosity. I don't dare try dreaming with him, but he might be able to explain things. He always seemed to have the right answers. He thought it through and his hope diminished. No way I could ever get into his dreams, besides, Elijah went out of his way to warn me of the dangers.

Then again I have accomplished some advanced things in dreaming, haven't I? Elijah said so himself. Maybe I *am* strong enough to deal with Mick. How could he be a danger to me? We were good friends while I was alive. Mick wouldn't hurt me – not willingly. He's my bro."

Without realizing it Steve drifted into Mick's bedroom but kept his distance to the point where the arkana was barely visible. He studied Mick's aura, mesmerized by it's bright blue radiance. It dimmed slightly, but still shone strong and its color remained uniform. Steve glimpsed at the point in the middle of Mick's forehead and a blinding light sent an intense vibration through his whole being before everything went black.

## CHAPTER FIFTEEN

Steve looked up into the concern look of Elijah's pastel blue eyes and felt his confusion subside. They were together floating in empty space.

"Elijah?"

"Are you all right?"

"What happened?"

"You're safe now but it's best to lie still for awhile until you regain your strength. That was a hell of a jolt you took."

"I don't understand."

Elijah frowned and shook his head. "I warned you about solid auras and the arkana but you went anyway, which shows you how powerful, dangerous, and seductive they are."

"But I kept my distance."

Elijah kept shaking his head. "You need to stay away completely. You need to go as far as keeping the very thought of it out of your mind. The danger to you has increased now that you've been exposed to its energy."

"But I didn't go near it. I thought that because my dreaming skills are more advanced than..."

Elijah wagged a finger at him. "Yes, your talents have set you off from the rest, but your limited consciousness doesn't grasp the bigger picture. I wasn't going to tell you this so soon, but because of the promise we've seen from you, you will be getting special training that is different from the others."

"We? The Masters?"

"Yes, but more than them, everything is guided by a higher intelligence that is both seen and unseen, all powerful, and ever pervasive. We are the instruments of its manifestation, which is what you are becoming more and more with each step of your training. We're worried about what's happened to you, so we're moving ahead faster than we had planned for your protection. Follow my lead." He disappeared, leaving Steve confused in the nowhere place with no up, down, or any other sense of orientation.

Steve closed his eyes and concentrated on Elijah. When he opened them he sat beside him on a bench in Balboa Park where they first observed auras.

"Very good!" Elijah smiled and nodded. "I called you here using my thoughts to test your affinity to me by matching the lines of force from my will to yours and putting a thought into your mind."

"Resonance," Steve said in a low voice.

Elijah smiled. "The secret lies in setting up the conditions to make it possible. I'm going to teach you how to do this with a mortal subject, but first we need to get you back to basics using the medium of dreaming to extend your influence on a mortal into the waking state."

He motioned for Steve to sit beside him. "So far you've learned to observe auras and enter into dreaming with people, and you have jumped ahead of the others and asserted your will on mortal subjects, even if only to a small degree. Now you're going to learn how to assert a stronger influence with a subject who won't infect you with tainted energy from primitive black magic. There's someone you know who will be perfect. Can you tell me who it is?"

"Jon!" Steve said without thinking.

Elijah brightened. "It will be a simple task to tune in to his thought processes because his involvement with drugs and alcohol have weakened his will."

Steve's thoughts shifted from confidence to confusion.

"Relax," Elijah said as if reading his thoughts. "The intention here is to guide him so he can become more aware."

"A spirit guide?"

Elijah winked. "Maybe even a guardian angel." He gestured like a lecturing professor as he spoke. "We're going to start by working subtly through his dreams and increase our influence until it filters into his waking state. I'll help from time to time, but you'll be the motivating force. We'll start by joining Jon in his waking state where we can pick up a lot of useful information, particularly his likes, dislikes, fears, interests, idiosyncrasies, and anything else that gives us insight into his personality."

"That's easy," Steve said. "Cocaine, weed, booze, and women."

Elijah patted him on the back and they materialized in Jon's living room a moment before he came in through the front door.

"Study his actions," Elijah said, "and watch how his aura changes."

Steve put his attention on Jon whose aura looked like a campfire moving in slow motion in red and purple hues that danced about his head. Steve thought it had more movement than others he'd seen, except maybe the kids.

Jon turned on his stereo, sat down on his couch and filled a glass pipe with some weed. His aura brightened with the first hit and dimmed when he took the next few. When he stopped his aura moved around in the same manner, but its intensity and activity looked more subdued.

Steve watched him listen to music with his eyes closed and saw his aura change along with the music. Hard driving rock and roll brought out more red, while mellower melodic songs accented the purple.

Jon went to the kitchen and popped open a beer. Drinking it dulled his aura more. When he smoked more weed and drank another beer his aura diminished further until he nodded off.

Elijah moved in closer to Jon and pointed to his head. "The idea is to bring out as much red as possible in his aura. It's a conditioning technique. You saw how certain things bring out more red than others." He gestured toward the stereo. "The amount of red you observe is an indicator of how much energetic stress you're applying, and the strength of it reflects the intensity of your efforts."

"It's kind of like blowing on a coal to get it to burst into flame, isn't it?"

Elijah tapped his head and smiled. "Exactly! If you stay focused and keep the pressure on while applying proper motivational techniques Jon's mind will resonate with yours in the same way your mind is now compatible with mine."

"Then what?"

"He will give in to the stress and do anything to appease your will." He held up a finger. "But sometimes he might do the opposite of what you want to prove that he is in control. In that case you have to stress him to do the opposite of what you want to get him to do what you want."

"Reverse psychology."

"That's one way of putting it. You have to understand his temperament by observing the results of your influence and working both sides of his impulses according to his moods to fully condition him no matter which way his emotions go. It all starts with dreaming which is on a subtler level of consciousness making it easier to work with. As we gain more of a foothold we can filter our influence into his waking state. Want to give it a try?"

"Sure."

They focused their attention on Jon's forehead together and directed their thoughts toward him until they came into focus walking down a street behind him.

"Watch this." A two by four appeared in Elijah's hand. "Don't be alarmed. No harm will come to Jon." He smirked. "It's a necessary part of his conditioning." Elijah crept up behind Jon and jabbed him in the back. When Jon turned Elijah hit him with the board, knocking him to the ground.

This is weird, Steve thought. I should be bothered by what Elijah's doing, but I feel indifferent.

Elijah turned and smiled a Cheshire Cat grin. "You don't care, do you?"

He's right. "I don't!"

Jon looked up in disbelief and Elijah let out a scream. Jon faded from view.

A moment later they materialized at Jon's where he stood by the doorway looking confused.

"Your turn," Elijah said."

Steve hesitated.

"Go ahead," Elijah urged. "You can't hurt him. It's only a dream. He needs to experience pleasure and pain with your help to condition him for further growth beyond his emotional extremes."

Steve shrugged, picked up a chair, and threw it at Jon, sending him flying into a wall. He stood slowly and looked at Steve, eyes wide with fear, then lunged at Steve hitting him squarely in the chest sending Steve reeling back onto the floor with no sensation of pain of any kind.

Remembering his karate, Steve jumped up and planted a kick to Jon's midsection and Jon faded out again.

"See? No harm and no pain either way," Elijah said. "I know it seems cruel to terrorize him like this, but it's only temporary to shock him into alignment."

They found Jon hiding in his backyard and chased him down the street until he faded again, then went back to Jon's in time to see him run in and slam the door behind him.

"Now for the grand finale." Elijah smirked. "This will wake him."

He produced a can of gas and doused Jon's living room, then struck a match to it engulfing the room in flame...

Jon sat up on his couch soaked in sweat with his hand to his chest, breathing deep gasping breaths.

"That's enough for one night," Elijah said. "We pushed him pretty hard. He's open now and you'll have more time to condition him further."

"I don't feel right about being so mean."

"It won't be that way for long."

They faded and came back into focus at Balboa Park.

"There's a danger of flooding him with too much stress too fast. We need to work on him gradually to keep him strong. Fear and violence are not the only ways to stress someone, but they are two of the most effective methods we have. As you progress you'll learn more subtle ways to influence him." Elijah nodded slowly. "After what we put the poor guy through here we owe him a reward. He's earned it."

"Hopefully a more pleasant one."

"I have to admit, in spite of its perverseness, part of me had fun chasing him, especially since no one got hurt, but it seemed like a waste of time."

"It's an essential part of his conditioning, and as I said, temporary. The anxiety it creates will carry over into his waking state and make him more susceptible to your influence."

Over the next few days Steve watched Jon in his day to day activities and discovered that different actions had different effects on his aura. When Jon smoked pot, drank, or ate, his aura dimmed. Any combination of the three had a more pronounced effect. When he indulged in cocaine or drank coffee his aura sparkled, making Steve think of a burning fuse.

On Saturday night Jon snorted two big rails of cocaine and drank more than his share of vodka. His aura became dominated by red and its intensity fluctuated rapidly. Steve waited, anxious to try another approach, but unsure of what it should be. When Jon's aura diminished to a more dormant state, Steve entered his dream to find him lying in bed. Steve stood by the door to his room contemplating what to do when Carla strutted in wearing a long red silk dress that clung tightly to her smooth curves. A slit in the side went all the way to her hip showing off her toned legs and the low cut top showed cleavage between perfectly rounded breasts that stood out prominent behind taut silk.

Steve watched, both confused and mesmerized.

She winked at him. "I think things need a woman's touch around here."

"What the fu…"

She put a finger to his lips, shushing him. "Pleasure time," she whispered seductively.

"Would you like to smoke some ganja?" Jon asked wide-eyed.

"No thanks." She looked him straight in the face. "What I really want is to smoke you."

She let the dress slip down her smooth figure exposing swollen nipples and ran her hands down her body moaning softly.

Jon's mouth hung open.

She licked her lips and climbed under the covers kissing him softly, her tongue flickering with each caress. Jon pulled her closer and returned her kisses with hungry probes of his own.

She moved against him in rhythmic motions, increasing her gyrations, driving her tongue faster and deeper. Jon wrapped his hands around her buttocks and she rolled on top of him, thrusting with her pelvis, building the intensity of her actions into a passionate frenzy until Carla arched backward and Jon let out a deep groan, releasing himself.

Steve watched awestruck, wanting her desperately despite the fact that he had no physical sensations or reactions.

Carla stood abruptly, put on her dress and walked to the door grabbing Steve by the hand on the way out.

"Don't worry, sugar," she said soothing him. "I've saved the best for you, but we have to wait until the time is right. You might find this hard to believe, but I did this for you. As you're learning, everything works in both directions through you, through him, through me, all connected and working toward the middle where it all comes together. When the time is right and everything falls into place, you and I will be able to have a complete physical union."

She led him out of the room and out of the dream.

"How did you know I was here?" he asked struggling to make sense of it all.

"It's my job to know," she answered smiling. "I'm your helpmate and I intend to do everything in my power to help you." She turned serious. "It's the least I can do and it's not totally selfless either. It helps me reset my own balance and make up for all the hell I put you through in our brief time together while alive. We're destined to be one." She smiled broader than before. "Twin flames."

# CHAPTER SIXTEEN

"This next part of your training may seem tiring," Elijah said to Steve while they watched Jon nodding off in a chair in his living room. It requires a lot of repetition, but it's the best way to master the technique."

"I guess the only way to find out is to give it a try," Steve said.

Elijah rested his hand on Steve's shoulder and squeezed. "We're going to influence Jon with food and music in his dreams and create scenarios involving them. The idea is to plant suggestions and reinforce them by repeating them over time. We can't give him too much at once and it's important to create pleasant experiences. By studying his reactions you can gauge how good a relationship you've established and when it's strong enough you'll be able to influence him in his waking state."

Steve leaned in toward Jon studying his dimming aura. "How?"

"By using a variation of your dream gaze with more concentration and will power you put more emotional energy into it. If you're successful his aura will react." Elijah stared at Jon for a moment making his aura flutter, then stopped and smiled. "You'll eventually be able to persuade him to act on suggestions you implant which will become familiar until he thinks they're his own thoughts, but it'll be your will he'll be acting on and you'll have a foothold that will pave the way for bigger and better things."

Steve rubbed his chin. "I think I understand what you're getting at."

Elijah graced him with a smile. "Good! Keep working with him and I'll check in with you when I sense you're making progress." He winked and faded out.

Steve spent the next few weeks manipulating Jon's dreams introducing food into them when he saw opportunities. When he wasn't working with food, he played Tom Petty's Free Fallin', Jon's favorite song, which made his aura flutter like a candle in a breeze.

Getting close, Steve thought after doing it a number of times. I wonder when Elijah's going to show up.

Elijah appeared as the thought completed itself. "I think you're ready to take the next step and from the look of things Jon has given us a perfect set up. Let's go into his dreams so I can show you how to make your actions influence him on a more conscious level."

Jon dozed off on his living room couch with an open bag of tortilla chips he had been snacking on and a copy of Rolling Stone magazine on the table in front of him. Elijah pointed to it before he and Steve faded into Jon's dream and found him sitting on the couch thinking he was still awake. Elijah picked up the Rolling Stone and handed it to Jon. "This is important, Jon. You need to read it. There's a great article about Tom Petty in it."

While Jon flipped through it Elijah pushed the bag of tortilla chips into his hands, saying "Eat. You love them!"

Jon took the bag without question and ate. Elijah pointed to the Rolling Stone again and played Free Fallin' on the stereo. Before leaving Jon alone with his chips, magazine, and music," Elijah said, "When he wakes up the first thing he'll see is the Rolling Stone. As soon as he looks at it focus your dream gaze on him. If you do it right the magazine will put his mind into the same frame of reference as his dream allowing you to implant your suggestions into his subconscious on an emotional level. If our programming is strong enough, he'll pick up the Rolling Stone, eat some chips, and put on the music which is the best tool for plying emotions. When you have the emotions you have everything." He smiled and they slipped out of the dream.

"While he's eating and reading," Elijah continued, "perform the dream gaze again with as much force as you can and think hard about Free Fallin' like you are actually playing it."

"That won't be a problem," Steve said. "We used to play that when I was in Triple Threat."

Elijah smiled, looking satisfied. "With Jon eating and reading like he did in his dream, your will power and emotion should be strong enough to make him play it." He held up a finger. "*And* he'll think it's his idea. If you're reaching him his aura will flutter. The red part is the place where your will can penetrate, so the more red you have, the easier it will be to resonate with him."

"What if..."

Elijah raised his hand, silencing Steve. "He's waking up. Get ready. Timing is critical."

Jon sat up on the couch rubbing his eyes and looked around until his attention came to rest on the Rolling Stone.

"Now!" Elijah said.

Steve focused on Jon's forehead and concentrated with all his energy on the thought of chips. Jon stared at the magazine and the red part of his aura fluttered, then he picked up the Rolling Stone and the bag of chips. Steve focused again on Free Fallin', losing himself in it like he had when he played it with Butch and Charlie.

Jon's aura flickered and strobed until he put Free Fallin' on and sat back on the couch with his aura fluttering to the music. Steve fell back drained and elated.

"You just performed what we call the trigger effect," Elijah said beaming. "One of the most important techniques you've learned so far." He pointed to the Rolling Stone. "We used that as a trigger which led to the chips and combined them to make a more powerful trigger for the music. By linking each trigger we created a chain of events. The challenge now is to form larger chains in as many different ways as you can think of with items familiar to Jon and lead to things familiar to both of you to put you in tune."

Steve brightened. "That's what we did with Free Fallin', right?"

Elijah beamed like a proud father. "Correct! By gradually inserting more of your thoughts you can make up more chains and set off the whole process with one application of your dream gaze."

"A domino effect."

"Your objective is to bring Jon to the point where he's thinking your thoughts are his, then we'll be ready to test your will against his which will strengthen his psychic abilities."

"Like a resistance work out?"

"Something like that." Elijah looked pensive and looked *into* Steve sounding admiring. "You really have a knack for this stuff. If you pass the test you'll be able to achieve the same results without any preparation in the dreaming state, but that doesn't put dreams out of the picture. They're still necessary to keep him open to suggestions."

Elijah rested a hand on Steve's shoulder and looked him in the eye. "Do you remember when I told you the key to influencing your subject was to reach them on an emotional level?"

"Yeah."

"Keep that uppermost in your mind. The sensual stimuli are designed to create an emotional response. Take food for example. Lonely people often eat to fill an emotional emptiness. They think they're hungry, but most times they're not. Music can have an even more pronounced effect. It's one of the best triggers we have and when used effectively it can set the emotional tone for the whole day. Going forward I want you to pick food and music you have in common with Jon like Free Fallin' and use them in his dreams like we just did to get into the flow of it, then you can build more chains and get him to eat food he's never eaten and listen to music he doesn't usually listen to. When you feel comfortable with that, see if you can influence him without going into his dreams and resonating with him, alternating between his dreams and when he's awake. I'll return when I sense you've mastered it."

# CHAPTER SEVENTEEN

Steve spent most of his time shadowing Jon and taking every opportunity he could to influence his dreams with things they had in common while bringing in more choices of his own to get Jon to act on in his waking state.

"I believe you're ready to test your will against Jon's," Elijah announced, appearing after Steve left Jon's dream one night and got him to follow through on implanted dream triggers after waking.

"You think so? I'm not so sure. Sometimes it seems too easy, and other times..."

"We have to choose our situation carefully to increase our chances of success."

"How can we do that?"

"We have to wait for a night when Jon indulges himself to set up triggers in a special chain and when he wakes we have to get him to follow it. The inner and outer chains acting together should put him in an enhanced state of receptivity."

A few nights later Jon stayed out late drinking vodka and snorting cocaine. Their combined effects made his aura low in intensity with a wide red streak that stood out stronger than the rest. Elijah appeared when he drifted off to sleep after he got home. "Everything's perfect," he said. "You ready?"

"Sure."

"In this dream I want you to talk Jon into taking a ride up into the mountains. I'll be in the dream with you. Jon won't be able to see me, but you will."

"Okay."

"Stay alert. At some point during your ride the two of you will get a surprise."

"What?"

He wagged his finger with a cockeyed grin. "If I told you it wouldn't be a surprise, but you'll know when it comes."

"Let's do it," he said, flowing into Jon.

Steve knew what to say and do, prompted by thoughts that he knew came from Elijah without knowing how.

"Hey, Jon!" Steve threw him his car keys. "Let's take a ride."

"Well... okay, if you really want to."

In the next instant they drove through the mountains. Jon looked confused at their sudden change of scene, but didn't question it. On impulse Steve put Free Fallin' on the stereo, making him smile.

"Reminds me of our Vegas adventure," Steve said, then he made his tone serious. "When you wake up in the morning you're going to take a *real* ride in the mountains."

"I thought this was real."

"This is a dream. Don't you think we got here awfully fast?"

"Yeah, We did. You're right. I kind of forgot."

Steve punched him playfully on the shoulder. "Tomorrow will be the real thing. I want you to set your mind to it."

"Okay," Jon said, nodding. "If you really want..."

They rounded a sharp curve and a man appeared in front of them. Jon swerved to the left trying to avoid him and heard a thud when his car plowed into their victim.

Elijah's surprise.

Jon stomped on the brakes bringing the car to a screeching halt. He jumped out and ran over to the twisted body. When he leaned over to check his victim the man reached up and grabbed him by the throat.

Jon screamed and disappeared.

He appeared lost in thought when he awoke. Steve continued focusing on him. Jon didn't respond until Steve renewed his efforts then he smoked a bowl of weed and his aura fluttered.

You have to take a ride to the mountains, remember? Steve thought.

Jon went out to his car with Steve following, keeping his attention on Jon until they drove east on I-8 toward the mountains.

Free Fallin', Steve thought focusing on Jon until his aura flickered and he put the song on. Jon tensed when they approached a curve like the one the dream accident happened at and Elijah's voice filled Steve's thoughts.

Concentrate on Jon with all the willpower and emotion you can summon and make him push his foot down on the gas. See how long you can make him keep it there."

Remembering his own experience with that same impulse, Steve focused everything into that one thought, reliving and re-experiencing it the way he had in life the same way he re-experienced playing Free Fallin'. Jon's aura fluttered and he stomped on the gas, flying into the curve. In the last possible moment he slammed on the brakes, screeching around the outer edge of the curve, barely missing the guardrail.

A flurry of conflicting thoughts and emotions flooded Steve and he blacked out, coming back into awareness exhausted.

Jon pulled the car over to the side of the road with a pained look on his face. "Whoa! Jesus! That scared the shit out of me. What the hell possessed me to do a stupid thing like that?" He stared at himself in the mirror.

Steve faded out again and found himself face to face with Elijah, torn between depression, accomplishment, and a peculiar sense of something missing, but he couldn't bring his thoughts into focus. "I'm tapped out."

"That's because you confronted Jon's will directly. It always takes a lot out of you, but you've proven that you're ready to prepare him for a resonance experience that will allow *you* to experience physical sensations again." His expression brightened. "Carla's been looking forward to that."

# CHAPTER EIGHTEEN

Steve walked along the curve in the road where his test had taken place to try and make sense out of his confusion. Elijah reiterated over and over again that asserting his will over Jon's was a big step toward bringing them into resonance, but the energy he expended had shifted something inside him, making his thinking and memories fuzzier.

Something felt wrong in the way it connected with the same experience he had while alive, but the more he pondered it the more scattered his thoughts became until he turned to see a van bearing down on him. He shrieked when it passed through him, leaving a series of chaotic scenes in its wake that ended with a van and a motorcycle flashing through his mind. He remembered looking into the face of a dead man, but he couldn't remember who.

Loss, emptiness, and confusion overwhelmed him until he sensed Elijah's growing presence flowing into him, replacing the vacuum and reinvigorating him like a fresh breeze clearing away storm clouds when Elijah's comforting hand rested on his shoulder.

"Your feelings are side effects from exerting such a massive effort of will, but they will pass," Elijah reassured him.

Steve wanted to accept what he said, but couldn't help thinking there was more to it. "Hassling Jon in his dreams, getting him to eat different food, and getting him to listen to music all seem harmless enough, but forcing my will on him doesn't seem right. It's like I crossed an invisible line of some kind." He looked deep into the pastel blue of Elijah's compassionate scrutiny. "What would've happened if my will had been strong enough to overcome his?"

"I know you don't understand right now," Elijah said softly, "but you're helping Jon!"

"How?"

"By stressing him. I mentioned this to you before. Nothing can grow without stress. When a body builder lifts weights he stresses his muscles and they grow as a result of that stress. To temper steel it has to be stressed by heat. Animals and plants grow strong and healthy due to natural stresses of their environment. That's why it's the strong that survive. By stressing Jon's will with yours, you not only make your will stronger, you make *his* stronger too and once you come into resonance..." His eyes took on a faraway look.

"What if Jon ended up dead?"

"If he were to die, which is highly unlikely, then his will to live wasn't strong enough to begin with, but if that were the case, he'd get an opportunity to retrain and reincarnate like you. No matter which way you look at it, he benefits. By working with him like you agreed to do in spirit before all this came into existence, you're working together to develop both your wills."

Elijah put both hands on Steve's shoulders and looked him straight in the eyes, and in that moment Steve felt something opening inside of him that made him want to do nothing more than please Elijah.

"You've been working with Jon for awhile now and it took a lot of work on your part to influence him to the point of motivating him to act on your thoughts."

"You can say that again."

"We're going to take a little vacation from him to give you both a break. Do you remember when I told you there were certain people who were easier to manipulate than others?"

"Sure. You said their auras were dimmer and the quality of perceptions through them wouldn't be very good."

He gave a single nod. "The experience you can gain working with them can help you cultivate more direct interaction with Jon." Elijah's eyes brightened. "We're coming to the part of your training where you'll experience physical sensations. We'll start with someone who is not very aware to give you an idea of what to expect from someone who's stronger so you're aware of the dangers."

"Dangers?"

"Until you're proficient you run the risk of being trapped in your subject's body. The only way to prevent that is to develop your skills beforehand. Let's take a walk in the desert."

With his hand still on Steve's shoulder they faded from the road side and materialized in the desert where the sun rose above the horizon. Steve marveled at the blooming desert flowers wishing he could smell the morning air and feel the soft breeze that preceded the oncoming day.

"We'll start with the baser physical desires." Elijah nodded in the direction he wanted to walk toward some low rolling hills, "but first we need to cover more basics to give you a greater understanding of what you'll be doing."

Now that they were moving and Elijah was in teaching mode, Steve's uneasiness diminished, replaced by an intense interest in what Elijah said.

"As you have been learning and experiencing, matter is composed of atoms that vibrate at different speeds. Lower frequencies represent denser forms like iron and lead, while higher frequencies represent lighter forms like hydrogen and helium. Matter is always a combination of mass and energy. If it is dense and low in frequency it contains more mass than energy and is more solid." He pointed to a large boulder to illustrate his point. "On the other hand if it is light and high in frequency it contains more energy than mass, and is more gaseous in it's manifestation." He pointed toward the sun, then to a few clouds scudding across the horizon. "Liquid is between these two extremes and represents a balance between mass and energy. Do you follow me so far?"

Steve nodded quickly, anxious to hear more.

"The human body is composed of varying degrees of mass and energy, but it's mostly liquid, so it falls in the middle. Exactly where depends on each individual physical makeup."

A rattlesnake slithered in front of them, oblivious to their presence. Elijah stopped and watched until it was out of sight and pointed to the boulder again. "The denser a body the more susceptible it is to the laws of matter, so it moves slower." He pointed to the sun and clouds again. "The lighter, or more diffuse, the more susceptible it is to the laws of energy, so it is more active. To apply this to what you're learning, the intensity and quality of an aura is a direct indicator of this. Slow, heavy mortals have low intensity auras, while quicker, high strung mortals have brighter, more diffused auras."

"What about us? Why can't we see our auras?"

"We have high energy high intensity auras that are so light that we exist on a separate plane of existence that mortals can not perceive. We can perceive them, but they can not perceive us." He pointed in the direction the snake had gone. "Like our friend who just passed by."

He paused letting the thought sink in, then, "We also possess the ability to control our rate of vibration like a radio dial that enables us to establish contact with mortals by getting in resonance with them. Your first experience with this was when you entered their dreams. While they sleep they're not aware of their physical bodies. They are in their astral bodies which gives them more freedom."

Elijah pointed to a tall cactus that stood atop a small hill and walked toward it. "What I've told you is the basis of how to act directly through mortals. We'll be observing their rates of vibration and tuning in to them. Once tuned in, all we have to do is vibrate at the same frequency to resonate with their unique radio station, then it's a simple matter to enter into their thoughts and bodies. Mortals who vibrate at higher frequencies are overly aware in a strange way. Due to their unpredictable behavior they represent a greater danger, so we'll start with lower frequencies. Once you experience them you'll understand what I'm talking about and you'll be ready to deal with higher ones."

They reached the top of the hill and surveyed the surrounding desert. The sun had climbed higher in the sky highlighting colorful spring flowers dotting the landscape. Though he missed his physical sensations Steve marveled at the fact that they had covered a lot of ground without breaking a sweat or feeling tired or winded. "Why don't we start with higher frequencies? Aren't they closer to us?"

"They're not higher in the stricter sense of the word. If they were they'd always be aware of us. It's true, some of them are to some degree, but they're considered mad or schizophrenic and often end up locked up if they get too out of control."

Elijah pointed to a hummingbird hovering beside a cactus bloom. "They're easy to spot. They're usually thin high strung individuals with erratic, super-bright auras." The hummingbird darted to and fro in flashes of beautiful iridescent colors. "The danger lies in the unpredictability of their actions."

"And the lower ones?"

"An armadillo lumbered out from behind a rock. Elijah smiled and pointed. "They're usually overweight, unaware, and their auras are dim. They suffer from sensual overindulgence and the lack of intensity in their aura is a direct indication of their life force. Anything they do to alter its flow makes them more susceptible to external influences and their energy is constricted and can't fully manifest through them, so they don't operate at full potential. They never really wake up."

He turned back to the hummingbird. "On the other side of the coin are high intensity types that dissipate their life's energy, literally burning up their life force. Insanity is common among them. To sum it up, the rate of intensity or life force expended by an individual is their burn rate. The lower ones are like smoldering coals that never quite make it to fire. The higher ones are like flash paper that has burst into flame.

Steve smiled when the armadillo scurried through Elijah. "What determines a person's burn rate?"

"A number of factors, among them diet and lifestyle. The more a person feeds their body, the more their body dictates to them what it wants until they end up following their body instead of their mind. The more they're into food the slower they become mentally and the less awareness they have. The majority of their attention is centered on food, but the more they feed their bodies the heavier they get, making them denser and vibrating at a lower frequency, then the slower body pulls the mind down with it."

Elijah went over to the hummingbird and studied it hovering inches from his nose. Steve marveled at the brilliance of its fluctuating iridescence in contrast to the gentle luminosity of Elijah's ethereal form before the hummingbird flitted away. "The high-strung ones are usually thin because their minds are racing ahead and their bodies can't keep up with their minds, so they tend to waste away. Remember, we're talking about extreme cases. Most people fall somewhere in between and possess varying degrees of these elements."

"Now I see why you want to start with the lower energies."

"They're much easier to handle and far more predictable. You're going to re-experience the physical sensation of eating through someone whose consciousness will be so lost in his food, he won't realize what's going on, but you'll have to pay strict attention. You can get lost in the food along with them, so I want you to go in for short periods at first. It's important for you to experience the food, but more important, I want you to experience what it's like to have a physical form again."

"I'll actually feel physical sensations?"

Elijah grinned broadly. "Once you encounter baser physical sensations, you'll be ready for the high strung types and experience thought and emotion on a physical level to get the best of both worlds, gross physical desires, and high strung emotional feelings."

"The physical and the mental."

"Exactly!"

"What are we waiting for?"

Their surroundings altered until they found themselves at El Torito's, Steve's favorite Mexican restaurant. Steve stood beside the overweight man he had been watching in what seemed like a disjointed dream from a million years ago that felt both foreign and familiar. How did Elijah know about watching him? He wanted to ask, but Elijah's instruction took his attention.

"Wait until he's indulging himself," Elijah said, sotto voce. "When he becomes lost in his food his awareness will be at its lowest point and his aura will be barely visible. That's when I want you to make your move."

Steve couldn't shake his uneasy déjà vu, and the more he struggled to understand, the more jumbled his thoughts became until the waitress came with the overweight man's food.

"Watch his aura," Elijah said as the man gorged himself, "The more he eats, the dimmer it gets. Keep your attention on it and start focusing your will until his aura reaches its lowest point."

Steve watched the man's aura diminish with each successive bite until it didn't dim any more. "I think it's there now."

"Concentrate on the red at the periphery of your vision."

"I see it," Steve said, watching it expand.

"Now wait until everything you see around the both of you has the same dull red hue."

"It's there now!"

"Good. You're in tune and resonating at the same frequency. In a moment you'll find yourself in his body. Once in, count to one hundred, break your concentration and will yourself out. Don't get comfortable. It's dangerous."

Steve felt the sensation of exploding in slow motion and expanding into the space around him. His awareness seemed to go off in every direction before he found himself inside the fat man looking out feeling lost deep inside a huge mass of spongy rubber. I can't believe this, he thought. I'm experiencing physical sensations again! He started counting mentally.

The first thing he noticed was the spicy taste and textures of a beef taco that made his mouth water. The stringy beef between his teeth added to the thrill of crunching onion, lettuce, and tomato, before sinking into soft cheese and sour cream. The fixation overwhelmed the rest of his perceptions. He changed his focus and became aware of his heavy, bloated body and felt gas rising in his stomach, then the pressure release of a loud fart.

His breathing came heavy and labored, his heart pumped wildly, and he sweated profusely. His efforts to move felt restricted, but the food tasted incredible!

Steve reveled in his sensations, then sat upright. Shit! Forgot to keep counting. He panicked and willed himself out until he fluttered in beside Elijah watching from outside.

"What do you think?" Elijah asked with a raised eyebrow.

"It's overwhelming."

"That's because his will was in control. Eventually you'll be able to be in control from inside him."

"I loved the food, but I didn't like his body."

"His life force is quite restricted. He'd make a terrible subject for long term resonance."

He patted Steve on the back. "Okay, focus in and do it again. It'll be easier this time, but be careful. "Don't stay in too long."

Steve focused again and flew back into the fat man's body. The speed of his transition startled him until the sensation of taste overcame him. Chicken. He stopped chewing, savoring the taste, mentally separating each component in his mind, tasting chicken and the spiciness of the sauce. His mouth tingled from the heat of chiles. He analyzed the textures of each component with his tongue, recognizing the difference between the tortilla, meat, and peppers and stifled a belch.

His thoughts moved slower than usual and he felt tired and burdened, then a deep sense of complacency enveloped him and he lost himself in the sensations until nothing mattered but the next bite. While wallowing in his sensuality a vague feeling of something wrong stole over him. He turned his attention back to his food and the feeling grew stronger.

He felt annoyed until he realized that he was getting swallowed up in the mass he inhabited. He panicked and tried to will himself out, but nothing happened, so he tried again putting all the concentration into escaping.

Things became fuzzy and he lost all conception of time while he strained to grasp some semblance of his former self, but it slipped away. In the distance he could barely hear a voice.

*Steve.*

He turned his attention toward it and it became louder, then he heard a loud "pop" and found himself looking into the fathomless pastel blue eyes of Elijah. He stared, entranced by their infinite depth. "What happened?"

"You indulged too much and identified with your friend. If I hadn't been here you would've been trapped at the mercy of your host."

Steve held up his hands. "No more. It was an interesting experience, but I've had enough."

"I don't blame you, but you have to do it one more time so you can control him with *your* will from the inside. It'll only take one or two suggestions."

"I'm not ready to go back."

"If you don't you'll be drawn to him by his will until the attraction gets stronger than you can handle and I won't be able to help you. All you have to do is control him for a moment. It'll be easier than you think, but the longer you wait, the harder it'll be. Get it over with while you're still attuned to his vibration. All you have to do is get inside him and concentrate on what you'd like to eat. Come back out while the waitress brings it, then get back in and gratify yourself. You've already experienced getting stuck inside him so you'll know what to watch for this time." He gave Steve a gentle push. "Go on. You can do it."

Steve focused on the fat man again and re-experienced the sensation of exploding in slow motion, immediately becoming aware of the aftertaste of a beef taco and the slow spongy feeling he had come to dread. When his thought processes slowed, he set his mind on strawberry shortcake and lemon pie and slowly became aware of the fat man's limbs and voice ordering them, so he left the body.

When the waitress came back, Steve focused and was back inside instantly. He didn't waste any time taking control and shoveling forkfuls of mouth watering strawberry shortcake and lemon pie into his mouth. As he feasted, he grew comfortable again, so he got out, still wanting more.

"Can I stick around and go back for more?"

"You've had enough. We'd better get you out of here."

"But..."

They disappeared.

# CHAPTER NINETEEN

Steve's world came back into focus beside Elijah on a bench outside the Balboa Park Botanical Building to the sound of a street musician playing soulful melodies on a saxophone on a little bridge over a long Koi pond. The distinct impression of strawberry shortcake and lemon pie stayed with him as a longing, and despite his fear of being trapped he wanted more.

"The longer you stayed inside your host, the more you identified with him," Elijah said after a few minutes of easy listening. "He also identified with you. He's been with that body for a long time and had the upper hand. The secret to avoiding those situations lies in learning to overcome the sensuality of your subject's body like when you took over and ate what you wanted. Once you can do that, you can take it over and use it for your own purposes. In the beginning it won't be hard. All the subjects we've chosen have weak wills. Do you understand?"

"Sure. I almost got trapped twice now."

"Good." Elijah patted Steve's knee. "That brings us to something else you should've noticed while in there."

"What's that?"

"Your last subject's awareness was much lower than yours. When you entered his mind your thoughts slowed down. With your next subject you'll have to be careful in a different way because your thoughts will speed up."

"High strung schizophrenic types?"

112

"You'll be dealing with more erratic thoughts and emotions. You'll have to speed up your vibratory rate to a level where you can tune in to a bright red shifting aura. It'll feel the same until you're in his body, then you have to be on your guard because the intensity of his thoughts will be so strong you'll want to identify with them. They'll make you feel alive again in a different way and that's where the danger lies. You can easily find yourself at the mercy of your host. It will be a different kind of struggle on your part to take control, but it has to be done, even if only for a second." He punctuated with his finger. "You've been through it once now, so you have an idea of what you're in for. The safest thing is to go in and out like you did before to insure that you don't get trapped."

Steve shook his head. "I don't want to go through that again."

"With practice you'll get stronger and the danger of getting trapped will decrease. Eventually you'll be able to come and go as you please." Elijah put his hands together. "But you have to take your big risks now. It's a critical point in your training, but once you cross this threshold you'll be on your way to freedom. Between this and your last experience you'll be prepared to tune into Jon in a harmonious energetic connection. He's almost to the point where you'll be able to flow into him and control his actions."

"With his cooperation?"

"In spirit, yes, but don't worry about that right now. You need to stay focused on the task at hand. There isn't anybody you know whose personality is compatible with what we need, so the best place for us to find a suitable host is right here." He pointed to the ground.

They faded out and faded in to a path in one of the park's remote canyons beside a ramshackle homeless encampment made of broken pieces of wood, plywood, and cardboard littered with plastic bags, shopping carts, bicycles, and grungy blankets. A thin man with short curly hair and glasses sat up from a bundle of blankets. He wore old grimy clothes and moved with short, jerky movements. His eyes darted from side to side as he clutched a portable radio and a plastic bag full of old clothes before starting up the path to the park.

Steve followed, focusing his gaze on the man and Elijah dropped further back. A bright red erratic aura danced about the man's head like wind blown flames.

"I've prepared you for this as much as I could," Elijah said, "but you won't know what it's all about until you experience it yourself. It's best to wait a few minutes to get a feel for your subject, then when you're confident make your move. I'll be watching. Remember, don't stay in too long. There's a danger of getting caught up in his thought stream."

The man shuffled along the path up out of the canyon until he sat down on a bench, suspiciously eyeing families with kids, young and older couples and the occasional person walking alone passing in front of him. When a lull came in the passersby Steve directed his will to the spot in the middle of the man's forehead. His energy field, already bright red, started filling the space around him, expanding until everything turned the same color including Steve who looked down at his hand and saw it turning the same shade of red as his subject's aura. I'm a chameleon, he thought.

Once again he experienced the sensation of exploding in slow motion as his awareness expanded. For a moment he thought he evaporated completely before regaining his bearings, then he felt his thoughts racing and scattering. His heart beat rapidly and his breathing felt raspy. He rubbed his palms which felt slick with sweat. It all happened so quick he became alarmed and left the body.

"All you have to do is get back inside for a moment," Elijah said, "and get him to turn his radio on. That's it. The radio will have a calming effect."

Steve willed himself back. Fleeting thoughts and unpleasant physical sensations gripped him and he struggled to keep himself from slipping into his subject's raging thought stream. Chaotic emotions assaulted him, but he steeled himself and set his mind to applying his will by concentrating on taking control until he felt himself animating his host's arms and legs. He fought back panic when a sour, pungent odor assailed him and he sniffed his sleeve. A wave of disgust filled him when he realized he was the source of the smell. He rubbed his hands on his pants to wipe the greasy feeling away, then looked at his pants and frowned.

What am I supposed to do?

He stood and turned on the radio which prompted him to walk. His thoughts ebbed and flowed with the rhythm until music soothed him, carrying him along with a power of its own and with each passing moment he slid deeper into a chaos that felt oddly familiar.

The C.I.A. are shooting electrons into my brain, he thought. They know I've met the aliens... No wait! It's the aliens! They're behind it!

No! Wait a minute. Those aren't my thoughts. The music took control of my thinking and sucked me into it...

He forced his concentration into leaving his subject, fighting back waves of conflicting emotion, but each one knocked him further back.

"They're after me. -- am – I can't make it. I – I'm dying. – supposed – Help – to do? – me!"

He shut off the radio and concentrated again until he lost control of his subject's limbs, once more becoming objective to his thought stream, then he reapplied his will one more time and popped free.

# CHAPTER TWENTY

Elijah appeared one night in Jon's dream and motioned for Steve to follow him out of the dream. "We have some preparations to make and the conditions are right," he said, barely able to contain his excitement. "You've become attuned to Jon and know his strong points and weaknesses, but more important you know how to create openings that allow you to get him to act on your suggestions. The one element we need to tip the scales in our favor will be present tonight."

"What's that?"

"A full moon."

"I always thought that stuff about the full moon was a lot of bunk."

Elijah nodded at Jon's sleeping form. "There's a lot of truth to it, but the knowledge has been distorted and blown out of proportion." Elijah went into professorial mode. "During a full moon psychic energy is at its peak and people are more prone to do things they normally wouldn't. Jon will be more susceptible to you now than at any other time and once you're inside under these conditions he'll always be open to you, but we have to use everything at our disposal, including the full moon to open him to the point where you can slip in and take over."

"How are we going to do that?"

"Using chains, only these will be different.

"How so?"

"You're going to plant thoughts that put Jon in mild emotional conflict and use chains to get him to take a drink."

Something inside Steve flinched, but he grinned in spite of himself. "That shouldn't be too hard."

"One drink will relieve the pressure he feels and make it easier for him to have another. Once we get him drinking we'll be on our way."

"To where?"

Elijah smirked and his eyes gleamed. "He'll get lost in his drinking to escape himself and the more he loses himself the more he'll want to escape, and the more he escapes, the less conscious he'll become. Nobody will be minding the store and he'll give up control of himself. If things go smoothly you might get him to create a little extra pressure in his life which can be useful at a later time."

"That doesn't sound right to me..."

"He'll wake up the next morning and won't remember a thing and you can have a little fun with no after effects."

"Where will his *spirit* be when I'm doing this?"

Elijah pointed at Steve. "Safe with you. You'll sense his presence, but don't pay it any mind and don't identify with it. You already know what kind of trouble that can get you into. Another thing to be aware of is that his physical body will still want to drink like it has a mind of its own, but the more that happens, the harder it will be for you to control him."

"I don't know, Steve said. "Something about this bothers me."

Elijah squeezed his shoulder. "Once you see how much fun you can have, you won't want to come back out."

"Maybe that's what I'm scared of."

"I don't think so. Jon falls in between the two extremes you recently experienced. This time you'll have more control. This is what you've been working toward all this time and it's for the greater good."

This last statement sounded like a contradiction, but Steve pushed it from his mind, thinking he didn't know enough and would find out more after the experience the way he usually did.

The following evening at Elijah's direction Steve started making simple chains with Jon as the full moon rose, then planted stronger suggestions in rapid succession. As Jon acted on one, Steve put another in its place leading him while never letting him settle on one thought. Soon Jon stood and began pacing. Steve filtered thoughts of loneliness that he knew all to well into the chains and increased their frequency until Jon's aura dimmed and Steve motivated him to play Free Fallin'.

The music dimmed his aura further and with little suggestion on Steve's part, Jon downed a shot of whiskey and turned up the music. After more shots Jon slouched back on the couch immersed in emotions and music. Steve kept up the pressure until Jon drank straight from the bottle making his dull red aura flutter in what looked like slow motion.

"He's primed," Elijah said.

Part of Steve rushed ahead, anxious to get in, but some smaller part held him back.

"Focus your will on Jon and watch his aura," Elijah said in a half-whisper. "It's gotten to the point where you should make your move."

"It's red," Steve said, "but different from before. It's fluttering — no, pulsating is a better word."

"You're tuning in," Elijah reassured him. "You'll be going any second now."

Steve felt his awareness "explode" for a moment before he found himself inside Jon. His thoughts slowed as if moving through quicksand, reminding him of how his own thoughts moved when he had drank in his life. He felt almost no resistance when he moved to take over Jon's faculties. His movements felt slow along with his coordination, which felt off, but he was in control.

He wanted to try everything at once – food – sex – booze. He stared at the bottle in his hand and took a gulp. The familiar full bodied taste of whiskey running through his mouth flooded him with nostalgia. He squinted feeling the after effects of its bite and smiled as warmth penetrated him.

I'd forgotten how good this is, he thought settling back in the chair letting the music carry his thoughts along until his desires multiplied making him feel frustrated and confused, then his mood changed from confusion to anger at being confused, stirring him to feeling obnoxious.

He downed another gulp and someone knocked on the door. He stood unsteadily and answered. A mild wave of shock went through him when he opened it.

"How're you doing, partner?" Jaret hit him lightly on the shoulder.

"Pretty good," Steve answered in Jon's voice, noticing the slur in his speech. "Where's Amanda?"

"Visiting her mother."

"Well, don't just stand there," Steve said. "Come on in. Have a drink."

"Don't mind if I do, but I can't stay long. I've got to meet some friends later. I just wanted to drop by and see how you're doing. I haven't heard from you in awhile, since…"

"Been kind of busy." Steve poured two shots and handed Jaret one, then on a sudden impish impulse spilled it all over him.

"Oops! Sorry about that," Steve said trying not to laugh.

Jaret's face flushed as he wiped himself off. "Forget it."

Steve felt another surge of trouble making energy flowing into him. He thought it odd, but pleasurable, like he was a little kid again.

"What have you been up to?" Jaret said trying to regain his composure.

"Partying," Steve said. He poured Jaret another shot. "How about you?"

"Working. I decided to get out and unwind a little while Amanda's gone."

"Where you off to tonight?"

"I'm supposed to meet some friends for a drink over at the Hard Rock Cafe in La Jolla."

"Sounds like fun. I think I'll join you."

An awkward silence filled the air until Jaret gave in. "What the hell," he said. "The more the merrier."

"Let's go!"

"Don't you want to change or anything?"

"Naw, let's go."

"It's still early. There's no big hurry."

"That's okay." He winked. "We can warm things up before anybody else gets there. We can do a little blow and take my car."

Jaret looked at him, puzzled.

"What's the matter? Don't you trust me?" Steve retorted.

"Sure, I trust you. I just feel like driving that's all."

"Suuure!" Steve said sarcastically.

Jaret frowned and a pleasant surge of mischievous energy filled Steve again, stronger than the first, like he was drunk right along with Jon. He enjoyed the feeling and wanted more. It felt like Jaret was giving up some of his life force and Steve liked the way it made him feel.

"Let's not make a big thing out of this," Jaret said in a low tone.

"Out of what?"

"Driving!" He said louder.

Steve felt a blast of energy. It *did* make him feel stronger and he realized that the madder Jaret got, the more he gave off.

"I'm not making a big thing out of it, you are!" Steve said goading him.

"Forget it. Let's go!"

They left in Jaret's car and rode in silence while Jaret smoldered with a suppressed rage that gave off a steady flow. Steve basked in the warm vibrant tingle it gave him.

I have to get him upset and make him think it's his fault, Steve thought, so he'll get madder at himself and give off more energy, then when he feels guilty, I'll zap him again.

Steve had a hard time walking when he got out of the car at the Hard Rock Cafe and stumbled. It was getting harder to control Jon's body. In spite of feeling energized he wondered how long he could keep his equilibrium. However long it is, he thought, I'm going to make the best of it.

A big, thick chested, bouncer with black curly hair and a goatee confronted them when they walked through the door. "You guys got some I.D.?"

"You've got to be shitting me!" Steve said.

"Sorry, but it's the rule," the doorman said keeping his cool.

"Well I think it's a schtupid rule," Steve blurted.

"Listen pal," the bouncer said with a change of tone. "I don't care what you think. Rules are rules and if you don't like it you can hit the pike."

"Oh yeah?" Steve said indignantly. "I suppose you're the one who's gonna make me."

The doorman looked at him wide-eyed, temper flaring. Steve absorbed every bit of it.

"Hey, Jon!" Jaret cut in. "Lighten up, will ya. Don't give this guy a hard time. He's just doing his job."

"He's just kidding," Jaret said. "Aren't you, Jon?"

"Sure man." Steve produced a driver's license. "Just kidding."

"Okay pal," the bouncer said with an air of authority. "But you'd better watch your ass, 'cuz if you get out of line, you're going out the door, got it?"

"Sure buddy." Steve walked past him.

"I'm sorry about him." Jaret handed the bouncer a five dollar bill. "Have a beer on me."

"What kind of dick move was that?" Jaret asked when they were out of earshot. "You trying to get us busted or something?"

"Did anyone ever tell you you're cute when you're mad?"

Jaret's face turned red and Steve drank in his essence.

"Come on Jaret, relax. Let me buy you a drink."

"Okay, but do me a favor."

"What's that?"

"Grow the fuck up and quit acting like an asshole!"

"Hey man, no problem. I was just having a little fun. If it upsets you that much I'll back off."

"Thanks, Jon," Jaret said. "You're a hell of a guy."

They made their way to the bar which was tended by a pretty buxom redhead in a frilly low cut red blouse that matched her lipstick. She smiled a perfect toothpaste smile.

"Hi, fellas, I'm Beverly. What can I get you?"

"If I told you," Steve said, "You'd probably have me arrested."

"I don't think so," she said casually. "Last I heard, they don't arrest people for overactive imaginations and undernourished libidos."

"That's it." Steve slapped Jon's money down on the bar and turned to Jaret. "I think I'm in love." He turned back to Beverly. "Darling, set us up with a couple of shots of Jack Daniels."

She poured and pushed two shots in front of them.

"Cheers!" Steve pushed one in front of Jaret and winked at Beverly.

Jaret gulped his and Steve ordered two more.

"Whoa, big guy," Jaret said. "Let's not go *too* fast. It could be a long night for us."

Steve grinned and pulled a little vial of coke from his pocket and nudged Jaret, holding out his hand under the bar so no one else could see. After that Jaret loosened up and they laughed and joked together like old times, the incident at the door all but forgotten.

Shit, Steve thought. I feel like telling Jaret who I really am, but there's no way he'd believe it. I might be in control of Jon's faculties, but I also have his voice and body, and they're – we're shitfaced!

He noticed himself losing more control. Even though his thoughts had slowed they still cleared after snorting coke, but after he knocked one drink over and spilled another on himself he knew his time was coming to an end. Out of the corner of his eye he spied the doorman staring at him from across the room, so he took the opportunity to make faces at him and felt the energy coming from him, knowing the man was on the verge of erupting. A group of people came through the door breaking the tension.

Steve saw by Jaret's reaction that it was his friends, so when Jaret stood to greet them, Steve staggered behind him, knocking over a chair. When they got to the door the bouncer blocked their path.

"I think you've had enough."

"Who you talking to, chump?" Steve lashed back. "I've had enough of you!"

"That's good 'cuz you're leaving!"

"Hey Jaret," Steve said with an air of self-righteousness. "Get a load of Godzilla here, he thinks I'm leaving."

"I don't think you're leaving. I *know* you're leaving." He grabbed Steve by the collar.

Steve tried resisting, but couldn't keep control over Jon's body Pulling together his energy, he focused his will and felt Jon's body fall limp as he left it behind. The speed that he left surprised and disoriented him.

He watched the doorman throw Jon and Jaret out of the Hard Rock. Jon was passed out. Embarrassed in front of his friends, Jaret apologized and reluctantly took him home.

Elijah appeared when they staggered in through the front door og Jaret's place. "How do you feel?"

"That was incredible!" Steve said, feeling the energetic glow in the aftermath. "Right after I got into Jon's body I wanted to cause trouble. I didn't know what I was doing, but it felt good."

"You didn't know what to do with yourself and the energy so you looked for attention and excitement because you didn't know how to deal with what you felt."

"I don't understand. How do you explain the anger?"

"The secret is not to identify with your subject's thoughts. You have to make them identify with yours. You learned that in your first experiences."

"I didn't realize it was so subtle."

"That's why it's important to pay attention."

"But what about the energy and pleasure I got from aggravating everyone?"

"Every time you upset someone their aura flared bright red along with their tempers." Elijah spread his hands wide. "If you had been out here with me you would have seen it, but being in a mortal body your perceptions were blocked. Even though you couldn't see it you felt it."

Steve nodded.

"I can tell by looking at you that you're saturated with it. How does it feel?"

"Like a dynamo. What am I going to do with all this energy?"

"Where do you think we got the expressions 'So and so aggravates the life out of me.' or 'He made me so mad I saw red.'?"

"Isn't it a bad thing to do?"

"On the contrary, you did them a great service by siphoning it off of them and relieving them of it so it doesn't consume them." He waved his hand. "By getting all you can, you're making a contribution toward maintaining the peace and balance of things which is an integral part of your work. Your purpose is to collect as much essence as you can. You've been doing it for awhile now, but you needed to reach a shifting point, a kick start if you will. In your dream manipulations and other day-to-day triggers you tricked your subjects into giving up their essence through pain and pleasure experiences. Now that you're coming into your own you're able to use more direct methods."

"Why didn't you tell me this before?"

"You weren't ready to do it consciously and you definitely weren't ready to hear about it. Now you've graduated to a higher level of spiritual power and with that comes the gift of healing by removing negative trauma energies from your subjects."

# CHAPTER TWENTY ONE

Steve checked in with Jon and Jaret the following morning to see how they reacted to the previous night's events. Jaret woke up first and sat on a chair next to the couch with his tablet computer and a cup of coffee when Jon sat up and rubbed his eyes.

"Well what do you know?" Jaret said. "The party animal man has decided to join us again."

"Please, not so loud," Jon mumbled, putting his hands to his ears. "My head hurts."

"I can't understand why."

Jon looked around blinking. "How the hell did I get here?"

"Don't you know?"

"I don't even remember hooking up with you."

"You serious?"

"Serious as a heart attack."

Jaret settled back in his chair. "Well if I did what you did I'd have a mental block too."

Jon closed his eyes and massaged his forehead. "What did I do?"

"You really don't know do you?" Jaret set his coffee cup down. "Do you remember anything?"

"The last thing I recall is sitting on my couch listening to some tunes and having a couple of drinks."

"You don't remember spilling a drink on me?" Jaret jerked his thumb toward his chest and put the tablet down beside his coffee. "Spilling the drink on me was nothing compared to the rest of the night. Once you got on a roll, you went into full asshole mode. Against my better judgment I took you to a club to meet some friends. You gave me a hard time about driving, and gave the bouncer a bunch of static about checking your I.D.."

Jon covered his face with his hands. "I don't think I want to hear this. I don't know what got into me. It's all a blank. What else did I do?"

Jaret sipped his coffee. "You kept aggravating the bouncer after we got in and you spilled drinks all over the place. I'm surprised they let us stay as long as they did. When my friends came you made a total ass out of yourself and got us both bounced." He frowned. "We're lucky we didn't get our asses kicked. You were so fucked up and out of it that you had me worried so I brought you here to sleep it off."

Jon rubbed his temples. "It's hard to believe."

"I've never seen you act like that."

"I'm really sorry, Jaret. I didn't mean to cause you so much trouble."

Jaret waved him off. "Don't worry about it." "That's what friends are for. I just hope you don't make a habit of it." He chuckled. "Besides even though you made an ass out of both of us, I had a pretty good time."

"I don't know what got into me." Jon looked puzzled. "I was feeling sorry for myself, but I don't think I've ever drank like that before. I've been on benders, but never to the point of starting trouble. That's just not me. The worst part is that I can't remember a damn thing. God knows what would have happened if you hadn't been there."

Jaret's brow furrowed. "You were definitely strange. What's bugging you?"

"I don't know. I haven't been myself ever since we lost Steve..."

"You weren't yourself last night that's for sure." Jaret drained his cup and went out to the kitchen, returning with it full along with a second cup he handed to Jon.

"This may sound weird," Jon said after taking a sip. "But ever since Steve got killed leaving my party, I've been having crazy urges and crazier thoughts. At first I didn't put much stock in them, but lately they've been getting stronger."

They both fell silent while Steve erupted in his own inner turmoil.

"Maybe you should think about getting some help?" Jaret said, breaking the silence.

"Sometimes I think about driving off the road," Jon continued, "or I get the urge to drive into somebody. Other times I want to drive as fast as I can, like I'm playing chicken with myself. The strangest part is that I know these aren't my normal thoughts, but they're strong!" He tapped his chest. "Like there's a war going on inside me." He sipped more coffee.

"I think you're a little confused, that's all. Don't let it get to you. Steve's death hit us all hard." Jaret's eyes went out of focus like he was looking at something off in the distance.

"I feel kind of responsible. After all I was getting him high that night..."

"You never forced him to do anything," Jaret cut in. "He did it himself. He was a grown man, accountable for his own actions. You've got nothing to feel guilty about. I feel just as bad as you and it eats at me."

Steve felt something shift inside like some mystery was about to reveal itself.

Jaret stood and went to the window with his hands clasped behind his back. "I wasn't going to tell you this, but now that we're on the subject, I've got a little confession to make myself."

Jon looked up, eyes questioning.

"It's kind of weird, but last night when I was getting crazy with you, it reminded me of being with Steve." He turned and pointed at Jon. "I almost forgot I was with you. You were acting just like him, and you kind of sounded like him, except you were being an asshole. I almost called you Steve a couple of times." He stopped and looked out the window again. "I wasn't going to tell you because I didn't want to freak you out."

"Maybe we're both turning into a couple of loony tunes."

"Maybe, but I think we've both been preoccupied with Steve's death." He lowered his voice. "Amanda too. It was a real horror show."

"I think I'm going to take this little episode as a warning to clean up my act. I've been having weird dreams too. I think it's time to lay off the booze and dope for awhile."

Jaret sat down again. "That's a good idea Jon."

Their conversation triggered flashes of memory for Steve, making him realize that his whole pattern of thinking had changed. Jon's descriptions reminded him of the thoughts and urges *he* had before dying, but he couldn't grasp them with any detail. When he struggled to remember they slipped away, leaving him with the feeling of having walked off a cliff into thin air with nothing to grab on to.

"Don't struggle with it," Elijah said materializing beside Steve. "I know it's confusing, but that's only because your spirit is shifting up into higher frequencies. Trust me here and I'll guide you through it."

"What about Jon?"

"Don't worry about Jon. He's coming with us."

Steve looked deep into Elijah's eyes and saw only serenity while chaos filled his thoughts.

"Don't struggle," Elijah said again, in a soothing voice. "I want you to use everything you have to get Jon to take a ride downtown tomorrow morning at ten. South on Broadway. If you can manage that, I'll take care of the rest and everything else will settle out." He put his hand on Steve's shoulder and Steve's confusion receded, replaced by singular purpose.

That night, Steve went into Jon's dream. "Hey, Jon," he said walking into the room. "What are you doing?"

"Just trying to relax."

"Listen, man. This is important. Do you see the clock?"

"Sure," Jon shrugged. "What's the big deal?"

"You have to take a ride downtown at nine-forty-five." Steve threw him his car keys.

As the night progressed Steve returned to Jon's dreams over and over again showing him his car keys and the clock on the wall.

He withdrew when dawn broke. Asserting his will so many times had drained his energy, but his singularity of purpose remained strong, driven by hunger for his lost energy, almost to the point of desperation.

Jon woke up at eight-thirty and glanced at the clock. Steve focused his will on Jon's forehead and tried implanting the thought:

Take a ride downtown.

Each time Jon looked at the clock Steve repeated the thought.

Jon hesitated in his movements, but it wasn't until his aura fluttered that Steve knew he'd succeeded, though he didn't know why it was so important any more, only that he was hungry and near panic. He stared into Jon's blank face.

Your keys.

Jon frowned.

Your keys.

Your…

"My keys," Jon muttered. He felt his pocket. "Where'd I put my keys? They have to be here somewhere."

For a brief moment Steve hoped Jon wouldn't find them, but at nine-forty-five he gave one last focused effort.

Go! Now!

Jon looked deep in thought, then his aura fluttered and he picked up his keys from the kitchen table and went out to his car.

Steve got in beside him and concentrated.

South on Broadway.

Jon took Pacific Highway to Broadway and drove South.

I don't know how or why I did it, Steve thought, feeling as if he might evaporate.

No sooner had those thoughts passed when a man on a Harley appeared from behind a parked car and pulled into their path.

"Shit!" Jon slammed on the brakes.

Something inside Steve gave way when he heard the thump and Jon froze, his hands clutching the steering wheel in a death grip. His face drained of color.

Jon jumped out of the car and ran over to the downed motorcycle. "You all right?" he asked, his voice trembling.

"Yeah, I'm okay," the man said slurring his words.

"You sure you're okay?" Jon asked again. "You don't sound it."

"Yeah, I'm okay," The drunk answered. "I think I jusht broke my leg, thass all."

Sirens blared and the authorities arrived a few minutes later. A crowd had gathered. Seeing the police and an ambulance at the scene of a motorcycle accident brought back painful memories that triggered a separation in Steve that made him feel like two distinctly different people. Part of him felt sorry for Jon, while his other side felt driven to act. The sensation only lasted for a moment before the urgency of what he had to do overtook him.

"Don't worry, buddy," one of the cops said to Jon. "This idiot's drunk. Fortunately, he wasn't seriously injured. No charges will be brought against you. Go home, relax, and take it easy."

"Thanks, officer," Jon said in a half-whisper.

After the cops and paramedics left Jon crawled back into his car, shaken. His aura shone bright red, except for one part – a blank spot.

As if on a remote control that overrode all his other impulses Steve focused on the spot and projected one thought.

You need a drink to settle yourself.

Jon stopped at the first liquor store he saw and bought a pint of vodka. Back in his car he took a healthy gulp and drove home swigging from the bottle and without further prompting he drank himself into a stupor. Steve felt his energy returning as Jon became weaker.

The feeling of separation stole over Steve again, more pronounced than before. His burgeoning powerful part felt rejuvenated and more in control while his quiet compassionate part haunted him like the ghost of a whisper. He didn't like the guilt and unhappiness that it brought so he pushed it from his mind and basked in the energy of his growing powerful side that drove him, motivated by an insatiable hunger, like part of him was missing and needed replacing.

"All right!" Elijah said flickering into view. "There's one more thing you need to do to consolidate your power before your mastery is established. You have to complete what you started, and collect more energy so we can move on to our rendezvous with Carla."

"Rendezvous? Carla?"

Elijah smiled and inclined his head toward Jon whose aura had diminished to a dull red that fluttered about his head. Steve hesitated, haunted by his own conflict, but the pressure to overcome Jon combined with the excruciating hunger for energy he felt grew unbearable.

He concentrated on Jon's aura, then on the peripheral area of his vision until everything became red and he expanded, filling the space around him. A moment later he was inside Jon, his mind filled with frantic thoughts.

My God, I could have killed him – It's my fault – Steve's dead because of me – I hate myself – Don't deserve to live – Kill myself – Need another drink.

He took another swig of vodka.

Steve wrestled with Jon's emotions, but was swept away. He asserted himself again and engaged in a battle of wills until Jon's resistance collapsed. Every movement of Jon's limbs took effort, but he stumbled out the door and made his way to the car. Realizing he was in no condition to drive he staggered down the street in search of somebody to aggravate to satiate his burning hunger. He went a half a block before a cop car drove by and turned around to check him out.

This'll be perfect,"he thought as the cop rode slowly past and pulled over in front of him. He got out of his cruiser and approached cautiously. "Say chief," he asked. "You all right? Maybe I'd better take you home."

"What are you a queer?" Steve asked belligerently.

"Listen buddy," the cop said, his temper flaring a little with his aura. "I don't have to take any shit from you. I'm trying to help you, so lighten up."

Steve swayed back and forth studying the cop. "Well, I sure as hell don't have to take any shit from you," he retorted.

The cop stood speechless, smoldering. Steve drank it in like someone dying of thirst, anxious for more.

"What are you, some kind of smart ass?" the cop said angrily.

"Better than being a dumb ass."

"If you don't watch your mouth you're going downtown. What's your name and where do you live?"

"Joe Schmoe from Kokomo."

"That's it!" the cop said. "Up against the car."

Energy flowed into Steve like a floodgate had been opened when the cop pushed him against the car, cuffed him, and took him to the station in silence while Steve taunted him from the back seat. The cop did his best to ignore him, but Steve fed continuously. By the time they reached the station Steve had charged up to his former level of energy and could barely move Jon's body so he left it passed out and watched the cops drag Jon to the drunk tank.

# CHAPTER TWENTY TWO

"We're going to take another short vacation from Jon," Elijah said. "We just put him through a lot of stress and the poor guy needs a break."

Steve felt empowered with an overabundance of energy that put him on edge that came at Jon's expense and he didn't feel right about it, so he welcomed the idea of change.

"It's a special place," Elijah continued. "Think of it as a training ground to prepare you for a special session with Carla."

Their surroundings shifted and when they stabilized Steve thought they were in a hospital until he saw bars on the windows.

"A funny farm?"

"Asylum is the proper word."

The day room looked normal for a place holding schizophrenics, but to Steve what he witnessed looked both morbid and fascinating. A toothless old man gestured while arguing with two wraith like spirits that glowed like Elijah. Two women in dirty yellow and white striped robes sat beside the television surrounded by other wispy spirits babbling to no one in particular. Other patients sat around the room in similar situations. Some of the spirits turned into "smoke" and flowed in and out of mortals like tiny vortexes. Others appeared to gang up on different mortals.

"What are we doing here?" Steve asked.

"We're here to learn," Elijah said. "Shift into your dream gaze and you'll get a better understanding of what's happening."

Steve squinted, changed his vision, and focused. All of the patients had predominantly red, multicolored auras that fluttered the way Jon's did before Steve inhabited him. Some spirits took turns going into different hosts. Others stayed with one subject.

Each human's face took on the features of the spirit possessing him and other spirits flowed into mortals like smoke being sucked into a fan through their host's eyes, ears, mouths, throats, stomachs, and genitals.

"Why don't they enter into the middle of the forehead like I do?"

"They're not as developed as you," Elijah answered, "so they go into lower energy centers which are easier points of entry.

Steve watched the activity and the quality of the energy and saw that the lower the spirits entered into a mortal's body, the more grotesque, deformed, and mindless they appeared and when he shifted his focus back and forth he saw two or more in the same body.

Mortals babbling to no one in particular had multiple spirits going into different parts of their body at the same time and their faces never stayed constant. Each time Steve shifted his focus he saw a different spirit's face superimposed on the mortal's in an eerie holographic fun house looking parody.

"A cast of thousands," Elijah said, confirming his observation.

Steve glanced sideways at him. "I don't think we belong here. The level of intelligence prevailing here isn't very high."

"That's precisely why we're here. As you can see by observing the auras of these people they all have low energy which makes them poor subjects for gathering energy, but their weak wills make them easy to dominate. They're also undesirable because of the inferior quality of physical sensation experienced through them, not to mention the distortion of perception that occurs."

"Why even bother? What good are they?"

"They're leftovers from previous manipulations that make excellent subjects for training. They're also cast offs from society who are schizophrenic, alcoholic, brain-damaged, psychotic, senile, and more often than not a shifting combination of all these." He gestured toward a mass inhabitation. "These undeveloped spirits are trying to get as much out of these mortals as possible. You could say they're fighting over the crumbs of whatever is left of their life energy."

"I know you didn't bring me here to watch," Steve said. "What do you want me to do?"

"Inhabit one of these inmates so you can gain a sense of interacting with other spirits through physical bodies in a group inhabitation to prepare you for advanced training with Carla."

Steve did a slow survey of the room. "The sooner we finish here, the better I'll feel, and the surges of energy I'm feeling now..."

Elijah wagged his finger at Steve. "Let's not be too hasty. You might come to like it."

"That's what I'm afraid of."

"There's a danger of lowering your vibrations and ending up like some of the spirits you see here. The more you inhabit these types of mortals the more you become attracted to their vibrational rate, but if you pay attention, nothing can go wrong." Elijah stopped and stared across the room.

"What is it?"

Elijah pointed to a bald emaciated old man sitting in the corner in a wheelchair. "See that old timer over there? He's on the verge of dying?"

"How can you tell?"

He pointed. "By his aura."

Steve shifted his gaze and saw it was nearly invisible.

"You can be sure he's been diagnosed with dementia," Elijah continued. "But what's really happening is his spirit is withdrawing from his body and he's becoming more attuned to our reality than he is to physical reality. He's different from the other people here. He can see us." Elijah waved his hand to encompass the room. "His mind is actually sound. It's his body that's worn out, but nobody understands that. He's afraid to give up his body but his time is almost over. I'm hoping we can convince him to come with us."

"Do you think we can?" Steve asked when they went over to the corner where the old man sat.

"Under normal circumstances I wouldn't do this while I'm teaching, but he's close to passing over and needs help."

"I'm not so sure," the man answered, studying them through narrowed eyes. "I can see and talk to you, but the doctors don't see you. They think I'm talking to myself but I know different."

"What do they know?" Elijah answered in a comforting tone. "If you ask me, they're the ones who can't see. I know you're lonely." He held out a hand. "Why don't you leave them and come with us?"

His eyes darted from Elijah to Steve and back again. "I'm afraid."

Elijah held both hands out in a welcoming gesture and shone a little brighter. "What's there to be afraid of?"

"Death." The old man's voice trembled along with his hands. "Are you coming to take me?"

"No," Elijah said, admonishing him softly. "We're not here to *take* you. We want you to come with your own free will. We're here to guide you."

"That's right," Steve added.

The old man rolled himself backward until his wheelchair was up against the wall. "I don't trust you!"

Aren't you tired of that aching old body?" Elijah said soothing him like a frightened child. "Come with us. We're here to relieve you of your burden."

"I'm no fool," the old man retorted. "I can see what's going on with these poor souls."

"You're not one of them," Elijah assured him. "You're just old and tired. There's no reason to cling to your wretched existence anymore. We can give you rest and happiness."

Steve saw a separation beginning and the old man's spirit floated up out of his body like a cloud of smoke. His spirit attached to his body by what appeared to be a fine, silvery strand of thread.

"There's nothing to be afraid of," Elijah said.

The old man's essence floated up further until the tiny thread strained close to the breaking point, indicated by what looked like sizzling sparks.

"That's it," Elijah continued. "Almost there."

The old man's translucent form flew back into his body as if the string had been made of elastic and a knowing gleam came into his eyes.

"Oh no you don't," he said with certainty. "I know who *you* are. You're one of the devil's disciples. You're not getting my soul!"

Elijah laughed and his soft glimmer disappeared. "Come on, Steve," he said in a monotone. "I was wrong. We can't help him. He's delusional."

The sudden change surprised Steve. The knowing gleam in the old man's eye and the conviction in his voice spooked him and he didn't know what to say or do. They left the old man alone, retreating to the other side of the room.

"Don't let it bother you," Elijah said. "There probably wasn't any hope for him, but I had to try."

"Don't worry about it," Steve said, trying to convince himself that it didn't. "I understand."

"Let's stick to the lesson at hand. You're going to be learning some techniques that will help you work with a group." Elijah held up a finger. "The first will get you into a weak-willed person in a minimum amount of time without using drugs or alcohol. Sometimes it takes a little prepping with alcohol to weaken someone who's strong-willed, but if the spirits you're working with are powerful enough, you can overcome almost any mortal using this technique." Elijah made an expansive gesture to the room. "None of the spirits here have that kind of strength, but none of the inmates have strong wills either, making this an ideal situation."

Steve glanced at the old man across the room who watched them through narrowed eyes, making him feel guilty and exposed.

"Don't pay him any mind," Elijah said. "Let me explain the mechanics of the task at hand." He pointed to himself. "Pay attention. Normally it takes three or four spirits. If the mortal can see you, then everyone starts talking to them at the same time. If they can't see you, then everyone takes turns implanting conflicting thoughts in their head." Elijah's eyes brightened. "Once they're confused we taunt them, then by watching their aura it's a simple task to slip in."

"Is that all there is to it?"

"There are variations. The difference lies in the approach." Elijah looked Steve in the eye and spoke in a low conspiratorial tone. "I brought you here to work with some old friends, but I want you to remember that your skills are superior." He held his hand up. "This is as far as most of them ever get. Your training has been more difficult than most and it takes special talent that most don't possess to withstand its rigors."

Elijah looked past Steve. "Here they are!"

Michelle, Rob, Lisa, and Mike materialized in a circle around them. Steve felt elated when he saw them and waited for Carla to complete the group, but she didn't appear.

"Carla's not part of this session," Elijah said, answering his unspoken question. "She's doing some special training on her own to prepare for you." He winked.

Steve felt disappointment at not seeing her mixed with anticipation at the prospects of when he would.

"Hey stud!" Mike extended a tatted hand. "Good to see you."

Steve shook it and Rob slapped him on the back.

"Hope you've been having half as much fun as we have."

Lisa and Michelle both hugged him.

"Sorry Carla's not here," Lisa said.

"But we're here for you," Michelle added.

"Rob and Michelle are going to work with one subject and Lisa and Mike will work with the other," Elijah said. Steve, you're going to sit this one out and watch while the two couples have a little contest to see who can aggravate their subject to the point where a manipulator can slip in. The one who gets in first has to hit their opponent's subject. Everybody ready?"

Mike and Lisa positioned themselves on each side of a short, stocky, cross-eyed man with wiry brown hair and began whispering rapidly in each ear until their voices merged into an unearthly harmony. Rob and Michelle chose a spindly graying long-haired, younger man with a wispy beard.

"I am Jesus Christ," Rob whispered in a light sing-song voice. "You have been chosen as the vehicle of my next incarnation."

"You have the power of God," Michelle stage whispered.

"I am Satan," Rob said in a low baritone. "Your soul belongs to me. You are my slave."

Steve glanced over at Mike and Lisa who said similar conflicting statements that escalated the agitation of the stocky cross-eyed man who argued with them until the volume of their voices raised. Rob and Michelle used their own tactic of goading and interrupting to spin up their subject, then the couples directed their arguments at the opposing subject until both men yelled at each other with increasing fury.

Steve felt like a movie director privileged to see and hear four professionals working behind the scenes to create a cacophony of escalating conflict between two people who appeared to be arguing with each other in the physical world. The ludicrousness of it all struck him as comical, and he grinned in spite of himself.

The two auras fluttered like wildfires while their red parts grew successively brighter until a blank spot appeared in the skinny younger man's aura. Rob slipped in and attacked the stocky man until two orderlies rushed over and grabbed him. Rob vacated the body, floating up through the top like smoke from a snuffed candle.

"You guys work fast," Steve said as the others floated back to him.

"That's only because these people are more than receptive," Elijah said. "Under most circumstances it's harder, but the interaction is not as direct. You have to rely on thought implantation to confuse them, but as you've seen, the secret lies in working together."

Lisa giggled. "That was fun!"

"All right." Elijah put his hands together. "We're going to help Steve get into a body, then help each other into bodies of our own to give everyone a chance to see things from a physical standpoint. By shifting your gazes, you'll be able to observe the spirits animating the subject's body."

He nodded toward a small, curly haired man with thick glasses and Mike and Lisa flanked him, whispering taunts in each ear.

"I am Jesus Christ incarnate. Hear and obey."

"I am Satan, Lord of darkness. Your soul is mine."

He screamed and grabbed his head. His already dull aura diminished further like someone had turned a dimmer switch down on a lamp and an opening appeared. Elijah looked to Steve and pointed.

This is too easy, Steve thought as he dissipated into the area around him. A moment later he animated the body immediately becoming aware of the man's thoughts.

Laser beams – They have laser beam eyes – They're after me-- Fuck them! -- They're not getting my pants this time."

Steve concentrated and experienced physical sensations, but his perception felt deadened like a dense fog hung close to his head. He asserted his will and took control of his subject with minimal effort. A sudden itch at the back of his head startled him, but the novelty of physical sensation pleased him. He scratched it slowly. Shifting his gaze back and forth he watched the rest of the group slip into other bodies and marveled at the contrast between the ethereal quality of his friends which were pleasant to look at and the dense darkened forms of their subjects.

"How're you doing Steve?" Elijah winked from within the shifting face of a skeletal woman with dishwater blonde hair. His voice had a slight reverberation that made it sound otherworldly. "Here comes a doctor. I think he's coming to talk to you. Why don't you have some fun and see what you can get from him?"

A middle-aged doctor with short salt and pepper hair and glasses strutted toward them, his lab coat flapping behind him.

"Excuse me Tom," the doctor said checking his clipboard. "It's time for your session."

"Who you calling Tom, turkey? Tom turkey! Get it?"

Elijah and the others laughed with Steve in a chorus of eerie reverberating laughs.

"Seriously, Doc," Steve winked at Elijah's shifting features. "What are you calling me Tom for? My name is Steve."

"Okay, Steve," the doctor said humoring him. "Let's go somewhere where we can be alone."

Steve held his hands up. "I'm not that kind of guy."

The doctor took him gently by the arm. "Don't worry, Steve. Everything will be fine."

"That's what they said when they put me here."

Steve let the doctor lead him to a tiny room furnished with a small table and two chairs with a mirror covering one wall with Elijah and the gang followed, so Steve stepped up his performance.

"How have you been doing, Tom?...er I mean Steve?"

"Wonderful Doc," Steve answered. "I love the view through the bars. They give me a real sense of security." He hugged himself. "And I can't forget the loving care I get from the orderlies, and the Thorazine really helps me think straight." He leaned back in the chair with his hands behind his head. "They going to let you start doing lobotomies again?" He put his feet up on the table and leaned back, balancing the chair on its two rear legs. "I'd rather have a free bottle in front of me than a prefrontal lobotomy."

The chorus of laughter from Elijah and the group echoed through him.

"I've never heard you talk like this before," the doctor said.

"Shit, man, I'm just getting started," Steve snapped.

The doctor leaned forward on his elbows. "It seems like you have some pent-up hostility..."

"What makes you think that?" You're very good to me. Where else can I get such good drugs?"

"We try our best to help," The doctor pulled out a pen and made notes on a clipboard.

"As long as you give us drugs then we're passive and happy, right? You're striving to make us normal members of society, but what's normal? Do you think the doctors and orderlies here are normal?" He leaned forward in his chair and put his face inches from the doctor's, glaring. "If these assholes are normal then why does half the staff have sex with the female nuts and what about the sadistic pleasure some of the orderlies get out of beating up on patients."

"That's not..."

"And don't forget the orderlies who got caught stealing drugs. If that's an example of normal behavior, I'm better off being a nut."

The doctor opened his mouth to speak and his lower lip quivered. Steve felt a pleasant tingle when the doctor's red flaring aura brightened, but he only absorbed a tiny bit of energy.

"You're obviously upset," the doctor said.

"Don't give me that shit, doc." Steve cut in. "I just spoke the truth and you can't face it. What are you going to do, zap me?"

"You're being unreasonable."

"Oh, well excuuuse me. I forgot. I'm the one who has something wrong with me. You're the one who's *normal*. I'm the one who's disturbed. Thanks for the reminder."

"All right, that's it!" The doctor stood and pushed his chair back from the table. "Go back to your ward."

"Fuck you!"

"Orderly!" the doctor bellowed. "Take him back to his ward!"

The door to the room opened and two big orderlies came in, grabbed Steve by each arm and hustled him out of the room. He heard the unearthly sound of Elijah and the rest of the group laughing along behind him. The orderlies manhandled him into the ward and pushed him down into a seat where he laughed until his stomach hurt before drifting up out of his host.

# CHAPTER TWENTY THREE

The energy he had gathered and his experiences working with the others at the hospital made Steve feel like he had topped off what he had. The power coursing through him felt intensified and the pressure to do something with it burgeoned. As he wrestled with it Elijah appeared, suffused with a soft luminescence, saying without asking. "Let's see what we can do about that."

How the hell did he know? Steve thought. Never mind. At this point I don't know which end is up. I want, but I don't want. I feel full, but I feel empty. "Before we start something's been bothering me," he heard himself saying. "During my life, especially toward the end of it, I felt like something was missing. After passing over, even with all the wonderful things you've taught me, I *still* feel empty. I'm not even sure what I'm looking for. Love? I don't know." He shrugged. "Whatever it is it's missing. Will I ever find it?" He looked into Elijah's eyes searching for an answer and saw compassion.

Elijah held up a hand and his luminosity brightened. "The emptiness you feel is the part of your soul waiting to be reclaimed. When that happens you'll be complete. You're on the verge of that now which is why you feel it so much stronger now." He looked at Steve, his head cocked to one side. "Your completion will come at consecration."

"Consecration?"

"When your soul will be resonant with the Lord's and consummated by a union with Carla, the gift the Lord has been saving to celebrate your homecoming."

"Homecoming? Is that what I'm starving for?"

Elijah answered with an enigmatic smile that lit up his whole face.

"I think I'm ready for that now," Steve said. "I feel like I'm going to explode. It's almost *too* much."

"Jon is primed and so are you," Elijah said, still smiling. When you reach Vegas you'll have to use everything you've learned and keep a sharp eye out. Carla and I will be waiting."

"Jon? Vegas?"

"What better place for a wedding?"

"With Jon?"

"If you succeed in getting him there you'll have passed the first initiation and you'll be ready to take the final steps toward consecration."

He disappeared.

Jon sat at home on Friday night smoking ganja and drinking beer. Steve sat down across from him, driven by a sense of urgency. When he focused his will on Jon's forehead his reaction differed from other times. Jon's aura fluttered in slow pulses when Steve sent him thoughts.

*Things have been tough for you. Time for a change.*

Steve felt his thoughts go directly into Jon's mind as though drawn out of him by an unseen force.

When he stopped Jon's aura ceased fluttering and when He started again Jon's aura reacted.

*You know how depressed and disgusted you are with life. You need something spontaneous and exciting to break free from the rut you're in. Why not grab a couple of grams of coke and some reefer and hit Vegas? A good blast will pick you up. All you're doing here is drinking and smoking yourself into a depression. A good snowstorm might be just what the doctor ordered.*

A short while later Steve rode along beside Jon watching the neon-like radiance the cocaine had manifested in his aura. After all of the things he had done with Jon previously, everything about this time felt super charged and easier, like the volume and brightness had been turned up.

Jon drove toward Vegas smoking ganja and listening to Free Fallin' over and over again. Steve looked to the East and saw a massive orange full moon cresting the horizon. His energy surged at the sight of it.

Jon snorted two rails of coke before going into Caesar's Palace that made his aura blaze before working his way through the mass of bodies to get to the bar. Steve sat next to him thinking, Something's got to happen soon.

His thoughts were disrupted by a belligerent voice coming from a burly lumber jack looking dark-haired man with a full beard.

"Hey, yo, bartender. Give me a fuckin' drink will ya?"

The man looked at Jon through glazed eyes. "What the fuck's happening dude?" He swatted Jon on the back.

Jon glared at him. "Nothing man." He turned away.

He jabbed at Jon's shoulder. "Don't turn your back on me, it's rude."

Jon's shoulders crept up and his eyes grew wide. He turned back. "Hey, pal. What's your problem?" His hand balled into a fist, his aura flared, and something shifted.

Steve saw the smiling face of Elijah superimposed on the lumber jack's. He winked and left the drunk's body in a wispy stream of pastel colored ethereal light, leaving the drunk with a vacant look. Jon took advantage of his lapse and walked away.

Steve followed him into the casino listening to the winning and losing screams and cries, and thought of animals in a dark primeval forest. He scanned the jumble of bodies in search of another sign alongside Jon who made his own survey.

Out of the corner of his eye he spotted an exotic looking young girl giving Jon the once over. Tall and slender, she had a lithe body and smooth tanned skin. Long, dark hair cascaded over bare shoulders falling almost to her waist. Her dark doe-like eyes and high cheekbones accented her striking beauty.

Something about her seemed familiar. When she looked in his direction Steve's vision shifted on its own and he gazed into the dark beckoning eyes of Carla. A surge of excitement drove him toward her. She smiled, slowly licked her lips, and winked seductively before disappearing the way Elijah had, leaving the girl to look past Steve before turning and walking away.

Steve scanned the crowd again and again until he became aware of a presence behind him. He wheeled around and spotted a middle-aged couple staring at him. The man wore a gray three piece suit, had salt and pepper hair and a handsome angular face. The woman had prominent breasts, a short red dress and attractive well-defined features. When Steve changed his focus Carla and Elijah nodded back, laughed, and disappeared in colored wisps.

Steve felt the presence behind him again and turned to see Carla and Elijah in their translucent spirit forms.

"What are you looking so surprised for?" Elijah said.

"How did I do?"

Elijah patted him on the shoulder, energizing him. "You have more to do but you passed your first test here."

"Which was?"

"I wanted you to sense our presence without seeing us. In the past I contacted you by tuning into your thoughts. This time I didn't." He pointed to Steve's head. "Instead we let you tune into us." He patted his chest. "You were a little slow but you caught on."

"It was strange. It started like an idea and grew until I turned and saw you there."

"You're not always able to alter your vision to see other spirits," Elijah said. "If you gazed all the time you'd see spirits all the time, but you'd lose whatever awareness you gained."

"Like batteries."

Elijah nodded. "It's part of the cycle of spirit energy that flows from the Lord into all life forms. Mortals give it off constantly." He waved his hand to encompass the room and all its activities.

"Instead of letting it flow into nothingness it should be collected and channeled back to the Lord. Up until now you've been learning to collect it. I'm sure you can feel it flowing through you." He touched Steve, heightening his sense of energy.

"That's an understatement."

"Now you're going to learn how to send it back through proper channels." He glanced over at Carla and they both smiled. "It's a very pleasant experience."

Steve longed for Carla and knew she was hungry for him. His thoughts accelerated and full realization exploded into his consciousness. "I think I understand." He looked at Carla who ran her tongue slowly over her lips the way she had before.

"We're leaving you again," Elijah answered, "but we'll be back with some hosts. Stick with Jon." His eyes brightened. "When we come back be ready to take him over and have some fun."

They faded from sight in a shimmer of colors.

Steve turned his attention back to Jon and implanted more thoughts in his mind.

*Have another drink. Come on lightweight. Get a buzz on.*

Jon went to the bar and ordered two shots of whiskey. Steve watched his aura diminish like the sun sinking below the horizon with each shot. After that Jon drank and gambled with increasing fervor. Steve stayed with him, watching and waiting and by early evening saw what he was waiting for.

The same dark-haired beauty he had seen earlier strolled onto the floor and looked directly at him smiling, showing her perfect teeth.

Steve focused on Jon and concentrated.

*Don't let her go. She's yours. All yours.*

He sensed his thoughts and feelings being directly communicated to Jon like it was being done for him by remote control. Energy pumped through him straining to get out and nothing mattered but the promise of gratifying his desires. His thoughts raced and he felt her dark eyes penetrating him, sensing his thoughts and feelings. He feared he might burst from the charged energy surging through him tying every part of him into one unified whole. His expanding thoughts and emotions all became part of the same dynamic force until he flowed effortlessly into Jon, bathing himself in erotic feelings that meshed perfectly with Jon's like a fine precision mechanism.

The first thing he became aware of was the thumping of his heart and the arousal in his groin. One thought. One desire.

"Would you like to join me for a drink?"

She slipped her hand into his and went with him without saying anything.

"Gazing" into the enchanting depths of her beauty Steve no longer had to shift his vision. He saw Carla like he had always seen her, only now he had a painful sense of urgency and a mild shock passed through him when he realized that this girl's spirit and Carla's were one just like Jon and himself.

He plumbed the depths of her eyes and she put her hand on his leg, giving it a gentle squeeze. A pleasant tingle shot through his groin. He leaned over and kissed her on the cheek. She smiled and patted his leg.

He felt light headed; the smell of her perfume, the warmth of her body. Breasts. It had been a long time since he thought about the soft breasts of a woman.

She caressed his leg and her dark eyes called to him in a seductive plea, giving him a throbbing erection.

His thoughts and emotions quickened adding to his physical excitement. His heart pummeled the inside of his chest and he trembled. He felt himself getting painfully harder as his reborn passions raged, then his animal nature became dominant and his physical sensations led his thoughts like a dog lunging at the end of a leash.

"I've been waiting for this for a long time," she said in a soft husky voice.

"You and me both," he answered, "I never imagined it would be like this."

"And to think," she continued, "This is only the beginning. After tonight you will have one final task to complete your consecration and you and I can be joined forever."

"Twin flames," he half-whispered.

She smiled dreamily. "This is a special night. One we will remember always. I want to prolong the ecstasy as long as possible. It makes it so much more enjoyable."

They spent time dancing and laughing, and as they moved together enjoying the feel of each other's bodies she rested her head on his shoulder and pressed her supple body close to his. Her closeness and the fragrance of her hair overpowered him and her rhythmic movements became more sensual and tantalizing. When she kissed him on the neck with soft wet kisses chills ran up and down his spine, driving him into a lustful frenzy until he took her by the hand and led her back to his room.

"Ooh," she moaned when the door closed, "I want you." Her kisses went from soft and wet to hungry and passionate. "I want all of you," she whispered. Her breath came hot and moist as her tongue danced and lightly probed his ear, wracking him with shudders.

"God, how I've longed for this," he said between breaths. "I love you. I can't stand to be without you."

His thoughts and emotions spun and his body trembled like a high pressure valve ready to blow. His erection ached. Carla stepped back and slipped out of her dress letting it fall to the floor, then she came at him again and undressed him, methodically working her tongue; exploring the recesses of his mouth. Steve moved his lips from her breasts back to her lips and down the side of her neck, caressing her with his tongue.

"Don't ever leave me again," he said. His breath came faster. "Promise me Carla. Promise."

"Oh, Steve," She moaned. "I want you inside me."

They fell back on the bed entwined in a passionate embrace and frantically made love. Steve driving forward hard with his groin, Carla answering with rotating pelvic thrusts. He put every ounce of emotion into his moves and felt the energy rampaging through him. Carla responded with the full force of her own primordial side and Steve reeled in ecstasy as the frenzy of their lovemaking increased. He felt possessed by a supernatural force when the final primal urge overtook him and his body shuddered in what was far more than a normal release and his entire being became a massive overwhelming orgasm.

A full on bodygasm, he thought in total surrender as all of his essence flowed into her. He glanced at the clock by the bedside.

Midnight.

Feeling totally drained, Steve fell into chaos. Panicking, he summoned all his will power to push himself away from Carla who glimmered with near blinding incandescence.

Trying to leave Jon's body turned out to be a struggle all its own. His essence felt depleted as though it evaporated like mist from a swamp. The exquisite tingle of pleasure had gone, in its place numbness and a distant feeling like – death?

"What's happening?" he pleaded. "My energy!"

"You've given it to me," she said, pushing him off of her. "Don't let it bother you." She smiled. "Go and collect more. When you do we can join again. It's the sweetest gift a girl could ever want. Thank you!"

She kissed him on the cheek, dressed and walked out the door leaving him alone inside Jon's unconscious body. Where once he'd felt incomparable desire, a numb, lifeless ache remained.

Elijah appeared standing over him, studying him. "Don't worry." He reached into Jon and pulled Steve out, helping him to stand on quivering legs. "You'll be all right. You're just experiencing growing pains. Once you achieve consecration you'll be strong again, able to overcome any obstacle in your path. Once you make your final commitment, Carla will become subject to you and you will be the one in control."

"What do I have to do?" Steve asked, fighting off waves of vertigo.

"It's very simple and you have to go through with it so you don't lose your life energy, otherwise you will end up like the lower spirits at the hospital, but trust me!" He wagged a finger. "Extinction would be a better fate."

"How could you let this happen to me?"

"You have to understand, this trial will make you strong and worthy of the responsibility bestowed on you. I had to go through the same thing myself. Now it's your turn to commit yourself to this task. There's no backing out."

"What do I have to do?"

"Do you remember the battle of wills you had with Jon?"

"How could I forget."

"You have to do it again, only this time you have to take things one step further and get him to follow one final urge from you." His eyes brightened with a frightening intensity. "You have to get him high and make him drive off the road, or into another car so he has a fatal accident."

"What?"

"You will be the keeper of his life force and guide his spirit when it leaves his body and train him in the same manner I have trained you. By this act you will be consecrated and become a disciple like me."

"But how? Why?"

"As I told you, you made this agreement in spirit with him before coming into the world, and now you will be fulfilling the promise you committed to back in that all encompassing time outside of time.

# CHAPTER TWENTY FOUR

The finality of Elijah's words haunted Steve with a choice he felt incapable of making, spurring his thoughts and emotions in frenzied rapid-fire explosions of mercurial indecision that bounced between two polarities.

Jon has to die.

No.

I can't.

I won't, no matter how weak I feel.

But I have to.

It's not right.

I have no choice.

No.

I choose not to choose.

His refusal made him feel oddly distanced from the two dissenting forces and in spite of the relentless back and forth he struggled to stay focused at the center.

He couldn't believe what he had heard.

"Do you remember the battle of wills you had with Jon? You have to do it again, only this time you have to take things one step further and get him to follow one final urge from you."

Elijah actually *said* that? Shit! And the way his eyes brightened. Scared the shit out of me, then, "You have to get him high and make him drive off the road, or into another car so he has a fatal accident."

I can't do that.

Elijah's voice responded in his head as if speaking of its own accord.

*You will be the keeper of his life force and guide his spirit when it leaves his body and train him in the same manner I have trained you. By this act you will be consecrated and become a disciple like me. You made this agreement in spirit with him before coming into the world, and now you will be fulfilling the promise you committed to back in that all encompassing time outside of time.*

I'm supposed to go through with this consecration, but I can't come to grips with the thought of doing something my heart tells me is wrong.

Something inside of him broke and his raging, polarized conflict crystallized bringing his inner compass to true North where the battle between his polarities took their places in the ground of their respective sources, his heart and his mind. He was in no man's land.

Take somebody's life?

He's given me no choice, his head urged. If I don't do it, it means annihilation. It's either obey, or..."

His rationality flitted away like startled birds.

From the start it's been against my conscience to manipulate people, his heart urged, much less take their life. Aggravating the shit out of them didn't seem right either, even if it does feel so good. He looked at his barely visible hand, aware of how depleted his essence was. His head took over.

Why should I worry about Jon? He's nothing to me. All I have to do is take his life and I'll have a new one, then I can train him to get his own. Do I have any alternative?

The details of his own death flashed through his mind and the tide came in again, bringing with it what bothered him. The old man at the hospital and Mick's solid blue aura ate at him. Something about them felt wrong.

His mind sped up, preventing him from thinking straight.

He clenched his hands together. "Please God," he cried. "Give me peace of mind so I can figure out what to do. I'm lost. All I want is the right thing."

His thoughts accelerated and grew more fevered.

Mentally scrambling for peace his thoughts went to Mick's power spot in the mountains, so he closed his eyes and pictured it.

When he opened them he stood among the pines overlooking the valley. The red sun below the horizon lit the predawn sky with a shimmer of silver and a breeze rustled through the treetops. He drank in the serenity and then sat down to try and forget his problems and enjoy the moment at hand. The beauty of it gave him some detachment and with that came a feeling of relief, and in those fleeting moments of freedom he no longer felt subject to his thoughts.

They became subject to him.

He breathed in deep and noticed slight pressure in the middle of his forehead that felt pleasant followed by patterns of flowing, swirling, colored lights that sent a muted twinge of excitement through him. His tension evaporated and a tranquil lavender colored light enveloped him coupled with a rising exhilaration he hadn't felt since childhood. It blossomed into a distinct presence, calm and peaceful, yet powerful. Words fell short of articulating his emotions. The closest he could come was pure joy, and even that was not adequate. He wept free and unashamed, letting go of everything.

Looking up through his tears he saw a beautiful ethereal being with gentle sky blue eyes that radiated understanding and compassion directly into his heart, expanding it.

His vision, if that's what it was, had long, silky chestnut brown hair, smooth olive skin, and radiated a soothing ultraviolet light that left him speechless with awe, trembling. At its peak Steve knew and understood her every thought and emotion. He looked deep into her eyes and understood everything without any words being spoken and in that one eternal moment total comprehension existed between them. Their communion could have lasted a second or a week. He had no way of telling.

In the presence of this beautiful angelic being Steve felt like a scared child who had finally found his way home and was now in the loving embrace of his mother. His thoughts jelled into one cohesive whole, and he knew in his heart that no matter what happened, as long as he put his faith and trust in this being, everything would turn out right.

It ended in the same quiet manner it had stolen upon him, leaving him alone with his thoughts, only now things were different. He opened his eyes and saw that the sun had risen above the horizon, lighting the sky as though broadcasting the promise he held in his heart.

He didn't know if his eyes had been open or closed the whole time. Had he fallen asleep? He had a moment of doubt and wondered if he might have dreamed it until a ripple of warmth passed over his heart, taking his doubt with it.

"Fuck that," he muttered. "I'm not going to do it!" They can't be serious about ending my existence. That's too final! There has to be a better way."

The sun shone higher in the sky bringing light and life to the landscape around him with chirping birds, buzzing insects, and the flashing iridescence of a hummingbird that hovered inches from his face for an interminable time, putting the dot on the exclamation point of the profound message he had received.

Anxious to put his conflicts behind him, Steve went back to Vegas filled with new hope materializing in Jon's room where Jon put the last of his things into his suitcase. He moved slow with slumped shoulders and his bloodshot eyes looked unfocused. His face looked lined and haggard like he'd aged overnight and the dull, throbbing redness of his aura reflected his physical state. In the next moment an urge to go through with Elijah's plan gripped Steve. The drive home would be the perfect opportunity to take him. They planned it that way, he thought.

He held tight to the commitment he made to himself in his visitation.

"Fuck that!"

Carla appeared as Jon finished packing his car still shining more than usual. "You may not realize it, but our existence is at stake here and I'm depending on you." Her expression softened. "In fact I'm at your mercy." A wounded look came to her eyes. "They told me it had to be done that way to motivate you to do the right thing."

He looked into her dark pleading eyes and she peered back into him, making him feel weak. He reached out to comfort her, but something stopped him.

"I love you, Steve," she whispered.

"It's not right to take somebody's life."

"My love for you is stronger than anybody's life. My love *is* your life."

Steve's previous thoughts and fears assailed him and he once again thought about going through with it when more intense conflict swept over him. Before he could think, the words came. "Carla, there's something I have to tell you."

"What?"

"There's a better way than this."

"What are you talking about? There is *no* other way."

"I went to try and sort things out. I didn't know what else to do so I cried out to God for help."

"You what?"

"I was answered!"

"You'll have to take Jon's life anyway," she said as if he hadn't spoken. "There's no way out. It's either him or you. You can't turn back."

"That's right!" Elijah chimed in from behind. "You have to go through with it. Jon must die so you may live!"

"Jon must die so you may live!" Carla said.

"Jon must die so you may live!" they chanted over and over again. Steve tried to block his ears but the droning of their voices caught him in a stupor that was impossible to resist. The eerie harmony of their chants split off into different voices in an invisible choir that crashed through his mind, shattering it like breaking glass. Waves of negative emotion drove through him and his body burned while his ears rang. He held onto the memory of his vision while his pain increased until the urge to take Jon's life gripped him.

As those thoughts passed Steve flitted back and forth between the opening notes of Free Fallin' filling Jon's car.

The chanting continued at a more frantic pace and through the din of it all one voice rose above the rest.

"All you have to do to find peace is go with the flow. Don't fight it! You can't win. You know what to do."

A flurry of dark confusion filled Steve and sharp throbbing pain shot through his entire being. He felt no pain when he went into Jon and it returned when he shifted back out. Each time he flew out the pain increased and the chanting grew louder.

His mind disintegrated, his sensibilities flowed out of him and everything reached a fever pitch until his in and out shifts came with such rapidity that he sensed himself in both places at the same time. His refusal to force Jon into action felt as though his whole being was pierced by thousands of white hot needles and his ears ached from the pressure of the chanting. He couldn't take any more, but remained steadfast in his commitment of inaction until his essence diminished and darkness swallowed him until he vanished into a black abyss and ceased to exist.

# AFTERLIFE

# CHAPTER TWENTY FIVE

After an infinite lapse of oblivion Steve came into awareness spinning through endless morphing kaleidoscopic patterns of multi-colored light with no sense of up, down, and no orientation to anything with any meaning. Only a sensation of falling, but it could have been in any direction.

The pain and chanting had gone, replaced by silence with no fear as he expanded infinitely into space, then flew back, collapsing in upon himself over and over again. Each time he came back he condensed into a smaller and smaller space until he squeezed into an area that felt smaller than a pin point before "popping" through on the other side where he felt only peace.

Am I really dead now? I can't be! I'm still aware of myself, but if I'm not dead, where am I?

Gentle patterns of swirling colored lights caressed him followed by tranquil lavender light that enveloped him with a rising feeling of exhilaration until he found himself suspended in empty space held by the flawless peaceful lavender. Nothing mattered anymore as he floated blissfully in a timeless limbo for what could have been minutes, days, or weeks. He had no conception of time and didn't care.

At some point his sensibilities shattered when he heard a hushed whisper:

*Steve!*

Its closeness jolted him. It didn't come from any particular direction, but it was a definite voice in his head.

*Don't worry,* the sweet sounding voice said a little louder. *You're not going crazy.*

Panic gripped him.

*Calm down!* the directionless feminine voice said.

He felt a familiar presence, calm, peaceful, and powerful that filled him with liberating emotions.

Pure love, he thought. His heart lightened and he wept, surrendering to the happiness and humility that pervaded everything.

Nobody was there, yet somebody spoke to him. In his mind. From everywhere. He never understood Spanish, but he had the uncanny sense that she spoke to him in Spanish and he understood it completely.

*You're right Steve. I know your thoughts. Soon you will know mine.*

"I'm not so sure I want to," he thought or spoke. He didn't know which and it didn't matter.

*Don't worry.* She laughed, sounding like tinkling wind chimes. *You will.*

At first her voice unnerved him, but now, he found himself attracted to it and it felt natural. "Who are you? Why can't I see you?"

*You can. It's just going to take some time for you to adjust.*

"Can we talk face to face?"

*Yes, but you'll find it's an inferior method of communicating. The way we're talking now is how we communicate here.* Her voice had a musical quality that Steve found enchanting, but he sensed it capable of great power.

"Where is here?"

*What you might call a higher dimension.*

"What do you want from me?"

*Only to help.*

A ripple of warmth passed over his heart.

"You sound like you know me."

*We've met once before.*

Through his tears he saw the beautiful ethereal being he had seen in his vision flicker into view. Her sparkling sky blue eyes radiated understanding and compassion directly into his heart, expanding it more. Her long silky chestnut brown hair and smooth olive skin radiated the soothing ultraviolet lavender that left him speechless and awestruck. Disbelieving what his eyes told him he closed them and to his amazement it made no difference whether they were open or closed.

Everything looked the same and in that moment he knew. Looking deep into her eyes he understood everything, though no words were spoken.

Once again her beautiful angelic presence made him feel like a scared child who had found his way home into the loving embrace of his mother. Joy welled up inside of him and a childlike curiosity played across his mind.

"What is this strange place?"

*A place to heal your soul from the havoc wreaked on it by the forces of darkness. We can go someplace else now. We have a lot to discuss.*

The calming lavender light faded leaving Steve and his stunning new friend in the mountains at Mick's power spot. He felt lighter than before like he still floated in lavender. Looking down he saw that his feet barely touched the ground. The trees and mountains shone with their own inner preternatural light and looked clearer than they'd ever looked; as though they'd been brought sharply into focus with a beauty and clarity he didn't think possible.

"I should've known we'd come here."

*I couldn't think of a better spot,* she said. *This place represents an important point in your existence.*

"How do you know so much about me?"

*You might say that you and I have traveled in some of the same circles.*

"With who?"

*Mick,* she answered looking him straight in the eye.

"Mick?" Steve's thoughts went blank and a new flurry of memories rushed in.

"How do you know Mick? How does he know you?"

She smiled wistfully. *We were introduced by a plant spirit.*

"A plant spirit?"

*Her name is Bobinsana.*

"Plants can talk? How is that possible?"

She giggled with her wind chime tinkle. *How are we talking now? We tried to reach you through Mick but you were distracted. *You have a lot to learn and much to do. You already have the basics in your heart. From this point on it will be a process of steady growth.*

"I don't even know your name."

*Teresa,* she answered with a disarming smile. *After your death your so-called friends took possession of your mind. They were after your soul – and they almost got it.*

Steve looked down still puzzling over his weightless form. "I know."

*But it wasn't entirely your fault.* She looked deep into him from behind her sparkling blue eyes. He never remembered loving anybody this much. *They deceived you at every turn.* She held her delicate hands wide, reminding him of hummingbird's wings. *While you were alive we tried reaching you through your dreams, but the vibration of your thoughts were too low and your mind distorted everything we sent to you in symbols that you couldn't remember when you woke up. Our thinking embodies universal concepts which can only be grasped in terms you call 'abstract'. Thoughts on the physical plane are like the thoughts of a new born babe in comparison.*

"I was so mixed up. I tried everything I could think of, but I couldn't help myself. It was too much too handle."

*You had the ability but you clouded your mind.*

She smiled beatifically and floated further up. Steve wanted to follow and as he thought it he ascended.

"Wow."

*Up until now you've been used,* she said. *You thought you had a choice, but you didn't. That's the major difference between the light and the darkness. You can be an unknowing, unwilling, slave of darkness who thinks they are free, or you can be a knowing, willing, ally of the light who *knows* they are free. The choice is yours, depending on the inclination of your soul.*

They continued floating out toward the valley like clouds.

Steve took in everything she said while feeling secret joy at the sensation of floating and the surrealistic beauty his surroundings.

*They knew you were more aware than most,* Teresa said. *That's why they tried so hard to get you. You'll soon see just how cunning and subtle the forces of darkness really are.*

"I've already seen first hand."

*You've only scratched the surface. The worst is yet to come.*

Her words jolted him.

*Once you understand their methods you'll be prepared to deal with them, only now you'll have access to infinite power.*

Steve bit his lower lip. "If there is infinite power available, why does evil seem to be running the earth?"

Her eyes brightened. *That's what makes our work so important. Evil appears to be running the world, but every soul has free will to embrace the light or the dark. Virtue can't be forced on anybody. To live in the spirit of truth and goodness, each of us has to accept that spirit freely into their heart.*

They passed over the mountains and headed east toward the desert. Steve followed effortlessly.

*Evil forces itself through fear and all its attendant negative feelings. Good isn't forced. It simply is. Evil exists to temper you so you can overcome it. We don't look at things in terms of good and evil. In our view reality exists in degrees of light and dark, the darkness basically being ignorance through fear. If you had to polarize it, it comes down to the fact that fear is contraction and love is expansion.*

"I never thought about it that way before."

They dropped lower and glided through the desert at a leisurely pace inches from the ground.

*You were a pawn in the hands of the dark ones who used you in a dark realm set up in a false hierarchy that is a reverse structure of the true order. The 'higher' you get in their order, the lower you sink and the more you crave to fill emptiness that can never be satisfied. Theirs is a world where the individual puts their own desires above all else.*

She waved her hand and they were back at Mick's spot where she continued speaking as though nothing had happened. *Each subject feeds off the one below who in turn is food for the one above. This chain extends all the way to the depths of darkness where they are all forced to steal energy from each other.*

"An upside down pyramid scheme."

Teresa rubbed her hands together and pulled them apart. Miniature bolts of lightning raced between her fingers as though she held a thunder storm in her hands. *We draw our sustenance from the boundless energy of the Source which is freely given and freely taken. Everything they taught you was calculated to fulfill your own selfish desires, but it is love alone that gives worth to all things. Upon your supposed consecration you would have possessed Jon and become a full-fledged psychic vampire!*

She threw her hands open sending a shower of sparks flying into the air. *They used their partial powers to lead you to partial truths. The only thing they're truly good at is twisting the truth to their own ends.*

"So much for reincarnation and fulfillment."

*You're not meant to reincarnate. You're meant to move up to a higher plane. The emptiness you've experienced is because you're incomplete. They played on that. Only the presence of unconditional love can fill that spot.*

"I thought for sure I was going to find it."

*They tricked you into indulging in your mercurial emotions so you couldn't think clearly. The more you were caught in them the more active your thoughts became and the more active your thoughts became the faster they moved, and the faster they moved, the further away from peace you went. Everything you did to Jon was meant to keep him in that state. What you didn't know was that the same thing was being done to you on other levels. You believed you were thinking and acting for yourself, but you were being used for their gratification.*

*Elijah and Carla lived through you to force you to lead Jon to his death, then you would have lived through Jon, while Elijah gained more power. Eventually, you would have trained Jon to do the same thing, and one by one the Masters would reel all your souls into the darkness.*

# CHAPTER TWENTY SIX

Teresa spread the fingers of both hands and wiggled them. *The real story behind energy is a little different from Elijah's version.*

Streams of rainbow colored light flowed into each finger out of nowhere which she molded like clay.

Steve clapped his hands like a delighted child.

*Matter, thought, and spirit are all composed of vibrations,* she said forming three balls of light that she placed floating in front of her, one on top of the other. *They are all energy manifesting in different forms. Matter is the lowest extreme.* She pointed at the lowest ball and it illuminated gold. *And pure spirit is the highest.* She pointed to the uppermost ball lighting it with a shimmering rose hue. *Thoughts and how we act on them fall somewhere in between.* The middle ball glimmered electric blue.*

Steve's thinking shifted and information came to him in abstract chunks that exceeded words. He faltered, then vocalized his understanding as best he could. "Thought is the manifestation of consciousness which can aspire to the uplifting heights of spirituality." The middle ball rose up with his words and merged with the highest ball, adding to its light, making it indigo colored.

*Or it can sink into the sensual morass of matter and desire,* Teresa continued. The middle ball sank into the lower ball, causing its light to dim to a faded blue.

*The choice lies with each of us and the quality of our thoughts indicate the proclivity of our soul.* The middle ball moved up and down between the other two. *We are the point where spirit and matter meet and there is an awareness of it. The very fact that we are conscious of ourselves is proof." The ball stopped in the middle and glimmered electric blue.

Teresa's abstractions filled his mind again. *Just like the polarities and gradations of light and dark. Hydrogen is at the high end of the physical scale and has the least amount of mass and the highest vibration.* The rose colored top ball grew smaller and pulsed brighter. On the other end of the scale is lead which has greater mass and less energy. They simply have different states of being, lead being more mass and hydrogen being more energy, but in the end it all balances out.*

Steve thought of all the colors, hues, and intensities of the auras he'd seen. Teresa clapped her hands and the balls disappeared, then she turned her hands sideways and opened them holding her left hand at the bottom and her right hand at the top. A shimmering silver ball floated above her left hand and a golden ball floated below her right under her chin.

*There is a struggle for every soul between spirit and matter, mass and energy, light and dark, good and evil, call it what you may.*

A smaller ball appeared moving between the other two pulsating silver and gold depending on which color it was closest to. *If we fall under the sway of matter.* The center ball fell into the lower one dimming it. *We become subject to gross physical bodies that will lead us into gratifying blind, chaotic, lusts. If we can overcome our ego with our heart, our spirit essence can lead our mind and body following a divine pattern of expansive revelation.* The center ball floated up into the higher one adding to its light.

*When you learn to master yourself, you learn to master the elements. You've already had experience with vibrations, but what you didn't know was that you were lowering your own and the vibrations of the mortals you influenced.*

Steve's thoughts moved faster. "If we're a combination of mass and energy and a person's aura is an indicator of their state of being, then the hue and intensity indicate their soul's proclivity..." He stopped mid-sentence. "Hue – We are beings of hue – Human beings! That's why solid blue auras created problems for my so-called friends. Solid blue represents a balance between mass and energy. That's why Mick's aura affected me like it did when I tried to tamper with it. And that arkana thing..."

*Bobinsana put it there to protect him,* she said matter of factly.

Teresa waved her hand and the balls disappeared. *Let me show you something.*

They faded from the mountains to the hospital where Steve could see both spirits and mortals without adjusting his gaze. A group of lower spirits taunted a wiry-haired old man and took turns going into him making him look like smoke continuously leaked out of him from different parts of his body.

Steve hid behind Teresa. "Why did we come here?"

*Don't worry. They can't see you. Your old friends can perceive themselves and mortals, but not us which gives us an advantage.*

Steve watched the ongoing inhabitation with increasing discomfort. "How can we watch without intervening?"

*They all have free wills whether they know it or not and were brought here as a result of their own choices. The lower they've sunk, the less aware they are, but they *always* have a choice. Their heart pursues them even in their darkest moments. You could have taken Jon's life. You didn't because you were free to make the choice, even a painful one.*

"Isn't there some way to reach them?" Steve held his hands out. "How did you reach me?"

*By transmitting my thoughts at the same rate as yours I made a connection and we tuned in to each other. It doesn't work unless both parties participate. Willingly.*

They faded out of the hospital back to Mick's spot in the mountains.

"When did I participate?"

*When you stilled your thoughts you found yourself in the sphere of the quiet center of creation and opened yourself up. Now that you know it, it's a matter of perfecting it by practice. Having the center as a frame of reference makes you relative to all. The only limiting factor is how much you can assimilate in one moment. You have the ability to expand your awareness infinitely.*

"You make it sound so simple."

*It is. You'll be re-tuning to the center by holding yourself in the moment and your consciousness will rise to higher levels. As you unify your will with the Source you will be met from the other direction. You've already started the reintegration process. Now it's up to you to return to your mortal friends so you can undo the problems you've caused and assist them in their growth.* She graced him with an enigmatic smile and faded from sight, leaving him alone with his thoughts and a sense of sadness at no longer being in her presence.

# CHAPTER TWENTY SEVEN

Steve felt a comforting serenity wash over him and knew it was Teresa by how happy it made him feel, then her voice filled his mind.

*Something important is happening with an old friend of yours. We need to hurry. Come with me.*

Before he could respond Steve found himself back at the hospital standing in front of the old man Elijah had been coaxing. Teresa appeared beside his wheelchair.

The old man's spirit floated above his body like a shimmering cloud of smoke attached by the silvery thread. A group of dark spirits pulled on him from different directions. His physical body twisted and an expression of terror contorted his face while the spirits moved around him in a frenzy. The presence of Steve and Teresa sent a visible ripple through them, but they couldn't see him or Teresa.

*Steve!* She said, shocking him out of his stupor. *Get on the other side of him and join hands with me.*

He did as she instructed, passing through the crowd of lower spirits and positioned himself on the other side of the old man, looking into the enchanting depths of Teresa's eyes when they joined hands. When they touched, her eyes shone with the same lavender intensity he had come to love, then she and Steve both illuminated with brilliant lavender light. Its brightness caused the horde to shriek in high-pitched terror. The light increased scattering dark spirits like wind swept leaves, leaving the old man's lifeless body alone on the bed as his thread broke in a brilliant shower of sparks. A peaceful expression spread across his face and a moment later he stood smiling between Teresa and Steve as a much younger man.

*Welcome home Frank,* Teresa said, returning his smile.

*Thank God!* He said without moving his lips.

I can hear him in my mind too, Steve thought.

They faded and rematerialized by a peaceful lake surrounded by tall pines and low rolling hills. A gentle breeze sent tiny waves scurrying across the surface of the lake.

We must be somewhere in New England, Steve thought.

*This was my favorite spot,* Frank said. *I used to come here as a kid and when I got older I came here to recharge my batteries.*

*I figured this was the best place to bring you after your little battle,* Teresa said.

*You figured right,* he answered. *I thought those devils were going to get me, but I wasn't going to give up.*

"I admire your strength," Steve said looking away. "But I feel awful. I almost helped lead you astray."

*That's why I brought you along.* Teresa said. *Your assistance helping Frank cross over made up for your past mistake and helped the two of you progress together.*

"Instant karma?"

*I'm happy you got the chance to do me justice,* Frank said extending his hand to Steve. *Pleased to meet you.*

Steve shook his proffered hand. "I don't know what to say."

*Now that we understand each other,* Teresa said, *Steve and I have to leave. It'll give you some time to adjust to your new way of being.*

*That's fine,* Frank answered, *I can use some time to myself. Take care and thanks for everything.*

"Same to you, Frank." As the words left Steve's lips he materialized back at Mick's spot, his mind spilling over with questions.

"Why does Frank speak telepathically? How come he didn't have to go into the lavender like I did? What makes him different from me?"

*Slow down,* Teresa said, giggling with her wind chime tinkle. *Your paths are different. In most respects you're more advanced because of all you've been through, but in other ways he's ahead of you. He caught on to telepathy naturally and he was blessed with the grace to forgive you. It was his forgiveness that released you both.*

Steve sighed, taking in his surroundings. The foliage, rocks and sky shone gently adding depth and texture to themselves as though they had a life and light of their own and their colors contrasted sharply. The combined effect calmed him.

*Frank's done a lot of wrong in the past,* Teresa said, *but he made up for it right up to his last dying breath. That's why we were able to intervene. The inclination of his soul at the time of his passing tipped the balance in our favor. After what you've done with me here to help Frank it'll be up to you to go back to Jon and apply what you've learned to help him. The more you can help him the more you'll grow, but you can't help him for the sake of your own personal gain. You have to give selflessly, regardless of what you think about yourself.*

"I'll be happy just to make up for my past mistakes."

*That's a good attitude. Helping Frank was easy because your involvement with him wasn't that deep, but working with Jon will be a bigger challenge. You did a lot to hamper his growth.*

Steve stared at the ground, embarrassed.

*Only by suffering for and with him can you grow, but we're not going to send you into battle empty handed.*

Steve looked up.

*Do you remember our discussion about being a combination of mass and energy?*

"We're all made of light." Steve held up a finger. "Human beings!"

*Our physical and spiritual bodies are batteries.* She waved her hand dramatically and a life-sized translucent form of Jon appeared.

*On a physical level it's the balance between acid and alkaline. On a spiritual level it's emotion and reason, or better still, the heart and the head.* She nodded toward the apparition of Jon. One side of it shimmered silver, the other a dull red.

*Bad diet, stress, drugs like cocaine and alcohol make a body too acid and bring physical discomfort and illness. Getting upset overloads it with negative emotions that produces more acid. Both create an overload of a negative charge that manifests as a red aura.*

She pointed a slender finger at Jon's stomach. Starting from the center and working toward the extremities, the whole figure glimmered the same dull red Steve had come to know well.

*As you've learned, the color and intensity of an aura indicates the state of that person's energy level. Elijah taught you how to increase their negative charge so you could drain off their energy and pass it on to the dark ones. By aggravating people, you short-circuited them and absorbed their life force.*

The red grew brighter.

*When you communed with Carla it drained you of the life force you had gathered.*

She snapped her fingers and Jon's form exploded in a silent shower of colorful sparks, then she waved both hands. A smaller, three-dimensional figure of the overweight man Steve had inhabited filled the air.

*One good thing that came from their training was that you got first-hand experience with the extremes. You saw how overweight people choke off their energy.* She made a sweeping gesture and the fat man metamorphosed into the street person Steve had inhabited. *And hyperactive nervous people spew theirs off into nothingness. One has too much mass with very little energy and the other has too much energy with very little mass. Neither has the proper burn rate.*

She swept again and Mick's image appeared, his blue aura shining beautifully. It's energy sent a warm caress through Steve's heart. *Mick is an excellent example of a healthy balance between mass and energy. That's why you were told to avoid him. The closer he gets to wholeness, the lighter his aura will get until it turns ultraviolet. He has achieved a high degree of balance between his physical, mental, and spiritual states. That's where we want to lead Jon. Mick doesn't know it, but he's one of us in the flesh.* Her eyes brightened. *By working with our plant brothers and sisters Mick has been charging himself with higher vibrations.*

Mick's whole body glowed the same as his aura, then it disappeared, replaced by the overweight man's image.

*His system is in a constant state of digestion so most of his blood goes to his stomach, giving less to his brain.*

The image turned translucent showing the blood flowing more to the stomach than to the brain.

*The less blood, the less oxygen, and the less awareness. By eating low energy, high mass foods, bodies build along the same lines. You end up with a lower vibrational rate and a lower level of awareness.*

"You are what you eat."

Mick's radiant image appeared again.

*Natural food and the rigorous plant diets Mick has done have strengthened his body with higher energy that brings him higher awareness that contributes to a healthier aura, better known as a glow of health. We want to work on getting Jon to connect with Mick on the physical plane so Mick can teach him and I can demonstrate things through Mick for both you and Jon. By observing how Mick and I work together, you and Jon can become a team like we are. We have to start gently. For now all we can do is present things to Jon. Nothing can be forced. We have to convince him we're teaching him truth, but he has to make his own choices with his own free will. Your challenge is to present things so that he understands that we speak the truth. Most people spend their lives rejecting it by running from the ugly reality they've created by escaping into food, sex, alcohol, drugs, cigarettes, you name it.*

An image of Steve walking through a casino in Vegas appeared in his mind's eye.

*What they don't realize is that it's a futile attempt to avoid reality, but sooner or later it catches up with them and the dark ones are experts at catering to it. They taught you to shock your victims with emotion to throw them off guard and they used you and your victim to gratify themselves.*

Scenes of Steve's key experiences with Carla and Elijah played out in front of him in three-dimensional holographic clarity.

*By getting their victims to act through feelings, the force of their emotions overrode their hearts. That's what we're up against.*

The images disappeared.

*Your task is to inspire Jon's higher essence so he willingly changes by giving up the emotionally based actions that make him feel alive. If he can deny himself he'll be filled with the loving presence of Source from within instead of the fearful chaotic presence of darkness from without. It won't be easy but at this stage of the game it's the only way you can redeem yourself.*

# CHAPTER TWENTY EIGHT

Steve floated into Jon's dream, sitting on the edge of his bed.

Jon sat up and rubbed his eyes. "What the hell's going on? You're dead!"

"We need to talk."

They faded out of Jon's room and materialized at Mick's spot in the mountains where Steve pointed to a spot on the ground. "Do you remember the night I died?"

"It still haunts me."

"I died under strange circumstances. A lot of what I'm going to tell you will be hard to accept, but hopefully you'll understand over time."

Jon held up his hands in surrender. "I know we partied together that night, but you ran out in a hurry without saying anything to me and I feel horrible about how it went down, but there was nothing I could do..."

"I need your help."

Jon looked puzzled.

"For us."

"Us?"

"If you join me we can work together all the time, but the only time you'll have any awareness of me will be when you're dreaming and it will be hard for you to remember. The rest of the time I'll be around. You'll have no knowledge of me, but the more we meet in dreams the more I can teach you and the safer you'll be."

Jon rubbed his chin. "This is all too weird. What's the catch?"

"The only catch is that you have to seek me out and I can only meet you half way. You have to come the other half."

"Why's that?"

"You have to embrace what I want to share with you. If you don't want to listen, nothing will be forced on you. You have to accept everything on your own terms."

Jon frowned. "I don't understand. What is it you want from me?"

"Forgiveness."

"Huh?"

"I'm partly responsible for the mess your life is in."

"How?"

"To put it bluntly you left yourself open and I took advantage."

"You?"

"That's why I'm here now. To try and undo the damage. I can guide us toward a higher consciousness."

Jon shook his head. "I'm *really* confused now. You say I let myself in for it, but *you* were doing it?" His eyes narrowed.

"You're headed in the same direction I was when I died and I intend to do everything I can to stop it, but I'm powerless without your help. It was through my own ignorance that I died, but what's important now is you. I want to help you become more aware so you're protected from the dark forces that did me in." He paused, letting his words sink in. "I'm here to help only if your willing to help yourself."

Jon glared at Steve. "How do I know you're not setting me up like you did in those other dreams?"

"You don't. You have to trust your own judgment and do what you think is right. The decision is yours."

His eyes softened. "You mean it, don't you?"

Steve nodded solemnly.

"I'm not sure I can trust you."

"Let me finish my story, then you can judge for yourself."

Jon nodded. "Fair enough."

"I was led to my death by a disciple of Satan."

Jon's eyes grew bigger. "Get the fu...

"I left an opening in my psychic armor he took advantage of, and was led down a path similar to the one I've been leading you on until my awareness fell enough for them to alter my thoughts and I died as a result."

Jon's hand flew to his mouth and he gasped.

"Once I passed over they posed as my teachers who taught me to gratify myself through you. What I didn't know was that they were doing the same thing through me." Steve put his hand on his chest. "If I succeeded in leading you to your death I would have used you in the same way they used me and you would have gone after your own victim."

Jon pursed his lips. "Things *have* felt out of control."

"It's an inverted pyramid scheme. The lowest man in the chain is the biggest victim whose miserable state motivates him to find a subject for himself, then each victim in turn is the subject for the one above."

"How did you escape?"

"By waking up, but I couldn't have done it without help."

Jon scrunched up his face. "I want to trust you, but I'm scared, man."

"The best I can hope for right now is to leave you with a spark of inspiration that the dark ones will try to extinguish. When you wake up from this dream all you'll feel is a glimmer of positive energy. The dark ones have you almost fully controlled, but if we strive for it, you and I can shift things in our favor. You game?"

Jon shrugged. "What have I got to lose? My life is in such a sorry state now I'm willing to try anything."

"There's a lot more I want to tell you, but our time is running out. The next time you realize you're dreaming try to direct your thoughts toward me. If your intent is strong enough we'll be able to..."

A loud buzzing permeated the air breaking up their surroundings like wind through a mist, leaving Steve alone at Mick's spot. The air shimmered like it had a life of its own and Teresa appeared floating above him. *You did great. It's up to Jon now.*

She floated down like a gently falling leaf. *You aligned your spirit with Jon's and flowed with him without forcing anything and the spirit in you communicated directly with his essence.*

She touched him on the head. *Your ability to open your channel will increase as you grow and more of the strength from the Source will flow through you. The amount of energy that can flow through you is proportional to the strength of your intention. All you have to do is set aside your personal goals and let the higher purpose flow through you.*

"I understand that, but there's something that bothers me."

*You were taught to work on getting Jon's aura down to a low energy level so you could slip in and create havoc, and the confusion you caused lowered his energy more. One of the reasons you got into his dream so easily this time was that his aura was low and you're wondering what will happen if he raises his consciousness and you're afraid you'll have problems getting in to work with him.*

Steve looked at her flabbergasted. "I couldn't have put it any better."

*If you're successful with Jon his consciousness will raise and his aura will grow stronger, and yes the color of it will change from red to lavender.*

"Will I be able to reach him?"

*His spirit will become more attuned to the will of Source working through you and merge with it while your will is also merging, so Jon will become more in tune with you which will make it easier for you to merge with him. Your energy fields will be positively charged and add to each other when they merge. Your goal is to help strengthen his aura until it shines like Mick's.*

# CHAPTER TWENTY NINE

After all they had been through Steve felt protective of Jon and spent most of his time interacting with him under a totally different set of conditions than he had been under in the lower realms with Carla and Elijah. Now he could only interact with Jon under conditions that came and went like weather patterns when Jon was open, receptive, and in a light-hearted mood. Nothing could be forced.

When Steve did visit with him in his dreams their experience had a lighter, more luminous quality that made Steve feel fluid and cloudlike. He often had the uncanny sensation of being both observer and observed at the same time without being drawn into whatever was unfolding within the dream the way he had in the lower realms. In this semi-omniscient state he offered guidance and suggestions to Jon, hoping that his influence would filter down into his waking life. His first indicator that it might be working came when Jon strolled down Newport Ave. in Ocean Beach toward the pier after much prompting from Steve, who felt a sense of accomplishment getting him this far, but he couldn't get Jon to notice the karate studio.

As if in answer to his wish a loud chorus of voices yelled "Keeyah!" in unison, causing Jon to stop and look across the street to see the huge tiger's head painted on the storefront window.

Jon trotted across the street and peered into the open door in time to see the class bow to Smokey and break rank. He paused in the doorway lost in thought for a moment and Steve directed his thought at him with all of the energy he could muster. *That's my studio! You need to study there!*

Jon frowned and continued walking down Newport Ave. to the pier.

Shit! Steve thought. Shit! Shit! Shit!

In what he started thinking of as his between the worlds state that Mick had called a powerful time, Steve floated in as Jon drifted into a fitful sleep filled with dreams of people attacking him with knives and guns.

*You need to study karate in Ocean Beach!* Steve urged him.

With Steve's influence Jon defended himself with karate in every case, his every thought and action executed with utmost confidence.

Feeling more accomplished and closer to his goal, Steve faded from the dream and in that instant a dark force jolted him into an alien feeling nightmare where Heather stood at the back of a crowd. He felt her terror as if it were his. The crowd turned and looked at her with accusing stares, then stepped aside, clearing a path to the front.

"Go ahead through," one of them said. "Take a look." It's your fault."

She put her hand to her mouth and bit at her thumbnail and someone pushed her from behind.

She walked forward, trembling more with each successive step.

The last of the crowd parted, leaving her staring at Steve's mangled body crushed beneath the front wheels of a van with his motorcycle, and in that moment Steve both saw and felt Elijah's darkness suffusing his broken body with inky darkness. Heather tried to turn away but an invisible force wouldn't let her.

The misshapen, blood-soaked thing that looked like Steve extricated itself from the wreck and shuffled toward her. One arm hung by a string of gristle. A white knob of bone poked through his shoulder and a single eye stared at her with soulless insanity.

Steve wanted to jump to her aid, but remained suspended between the worlds, forced to watch the unfolding horror, helpless to act.

"It's your fault," it croaked through bloody, shattered teeth. "Because of you, bitch. I'm dead." His one good arm grabbed her by the throat. "You're coming with me!" it growled.

She screamed silent at first, followed by a full-throated scream that popped Steve out of the dream into her room.

She woke up glistening with sweat. Her wide-eyed terror took a few seconds to come into focus. "The only memories I want of him are the happier ones," she whispered, but the more I struggle the stronger it gets. I need to talk to someone, but who?"

Without knowing where the impulse came from, Steve put the full force of his emotion into one thought, knowing it was the right one.

*Jon!*

Jumping as if actually hearing Steve's voice, Heather dug through her bedside table drawer and came up with a tattered piece of paper with Jon's number scrawled on it in Steve's handwriting. She studied it for a minute, then picked up her cell phone and tapped in the number, then disconnected before it could ring. She stared at it, then punched in the number again, disconnecting after two rings and putting it down. She appeared lost in thought, then grabbed a prescription bottle and shook out two Valium.

# CHAPTER THIRTY

Steve felt drawn back to Jon by a force outside of him in time to see Jon hurry out the door. When he reached the street his cell phone rang. He hit the icon and put the phone to his ear, but the line was silent. He looked at the screen and didn't recognize the number. "Fucking spammers."

Though he had been attracted to Jon by an unseen force, it had a different energy that Steve sensed he could break away from, which meant he had a choice. The sensation of being carried along by something outside of him that was not forced felt exquisite, so he accepted it as guidance from Teresa with no further doubt or question.

To his joy and surprise Jon drove straight to the karate studio and went in as two brown belts squared off. He took a seat by the door and watched them move around each other exchanging volleys of kicks and punches. As usual, Smokey moved light on his feet, speaking softly while charging the atmosphere with authority. He acknowledged Jon with a nod and a glance before turning his attention back to the combatants.

After a few minutes of spirited fighting, Smokey stepped in, commanding, "Break!"

The The brown belts stopped sparring, bowed to him and bowed to each other.

Jon watched fascinated as different combinations of colored belts fought while Steve oversaw all of it with a deep longing at his inability to connect with his old friends, but he also felt proud to see that many of them had advanced in rank.

When it was over they lined up according to rank, did a series of punches from the hip, then bowed to Smokey, leaving Steve feeling more nostalgic than ever. After shaking hands with his students, Smokey approached Jon.

"Can I help you?"

"I'd like to see about taking lessons," Jon said.

"What's your name?"

"Jon."

"My name's Smokey." He gave Jon a firm handshake. "Come on into my office and I'll explain our program to you."

I can't believe it, Steve thought. We did it!

*We sure did,* Teresa said in his mind. *That was the easy part, but it's only the beginning and we don't have much time. Carla and Elijah are making plans and your true test is yet to come.*

Their surroundings blurred but her voice remained constant while Mick's spot came into focus. *Even though Carla and Elijah think you're gone, the focus of their assault will be directed toward those you have been been emotionally connected to, especially those who feel the most isolated and alone.*

Heather, he thought. "If they want a fight, they'll get one."

*That's exactly what they want.* Teresa said. *The only way to overcome them is with love. The darkness wants you to struggle so you'll give up your energy. You have to hold fast and overcome them through love.* Her communication shifted as though coming from another place. *Accustom yourself continually to make many acts of love, for they enkindle and melt the soul. The love you give will be an extension of the Source, the only thing that can oppose the projection of their darkness.*

She looked into Steve with a loving gaze. *Don't react to the darkness living through them. Shine your light on it within them.* Her luminescence grew, projecting a comforting warmth before subsiding. *This as an opportunity to act as a channel from Source. By letting the dark ones attack you at your weakest point and returning it with love you can become stronger and your character will be rounded in a way that will raise you to a higher consciousness.* She smiled dreamily. *This is not only a test for you, it's a test for Jon.*

"What about you?"

*I can counsel you and provide you with spiritual energy, but the test is for you and Jon. No matter what happens, if you abandon yourself to what is right and true in each moment, even when all seems lost, the power from Source will come through.* She turned her palms up and they glimmered with lavender light.

"How can I prepare?"

*Continue working with Jon. I have no doubt that Mick will sense his spirit and guide Jon on the physical plane to help him rediscover what he's been taught by you while in his heightened states of dreaming. Hopefully, with Mick's help, Jon will be able to bring them to light in his waking state. The sooner he can get in touch with it the better. I can feel something coming. We can never tell when or how it will manifest so all we can do is prepare.*

# CHAPTER THIRTY ONE

Steve felt thrilled, nostalgic, and saddened watching Jon's first sparring class. Jon never saw the first punch coming, but it hit him between the eyes and everything he did looked awkward and out of time compared to the ease with which brown-belted Mick moved.

"Okay, Jon," Smokey said from behind him, "settle down and relax. That's it Mick, work with him."

Mick smiled and winked at Smokey before unloading on Jon with a combination punch. Its explosiveness startled Jon and struck hard enough to let him know he'd been hit without hurting him. After a few more minutes Smokey stopped the bout and told them to sit down. Mick extended his gloved hand which Jon shook timidly.

They spent the rest of the class watching others spar and when the class ended Smokey introduced Jon. Each of them came up one by one and introduced himself. Mick came up last.

"My name's Mick," he said extending his hand.

"Jon." He studied Mick for an uncomfortable moment.

This is it, Steve thought. *Say it!*

"Something on your mind?" Mick said, studying Jon.

"Well, uh," he stammered. "I think your reputation precedes you."

Mick's eyebrows raised. "Do tell."

Jon lowered his head and spoke softer. "My buddy Steve used to come here. He talked about you a lot." He looked up meeting Mick's gaze. "He really thought a lot of you. Said you were teaching him things."

Mick blinked like he'd been hit and Steve felt the emotional exchange between them in the short silence that followed.

"Steve was a good guy," Mick said. "We did a bit of riding together." He gave a half smile and his eyes took on a far away look. "And we had a bit of fun pounding on each other here before his accident."

Jon looked down again and slowly shook his head. "I was there the night it happened. In fact he was leaving a party at my place..." His voice faded almost to a whisper.

Mick clapped him on the shoulder and Jon looked up again.

"Listen," Mick said. "That hit us all hard." He nodded. "Any friend of Steve's is a friend of mine, so if you ever need to talk I'm at your service." He snapped a sharp salute and Steve felt his heart lighten.

Jon smiled sheepishly. "I just might take you up on that."

"Nice meeting you." He shook Jon's hand again. "Sorry, but I have to run right now. See you soon."

"Okay."

Steve watched Jon lay back on his pillow that night and drift into the first layers of sleep. He was about to try slipping into Jon's dream when his phone rang making them both jump.

It rang twice before Jon picked it up and hit the answer icon. "Jon's pool hall. Eight ball speaking."

"Jon?"

On hearing Heather's voice Steve's awareness shifted and he found himself both at Heather's side and still with Jon, *fully aware of being in both places at the same time* with no sense of any discontinuity or split. It was all one.

"It's Heather."

"Heather?" Jon nearly dropped the phone. His hand shook.

"I was afraid you wouldn't remember."

"How could I forget?"

"How are you doing?" Jon continued. "I haven't seen you since Steve – died. Where have you been?"

"Around. Sort of. I've been keeping to myself. Excuse me for being so blunt, but I needed to talk to someone."

"What's wrong?" Heather broke down sobbing and Steve felt a sinking feeling that pained him.

"Take it easy," Jon managed. "We can talk all you want."

After a strained silence Heather spoke between sobs. "I was hoping we could talk face to face. Talking over the phone seems impersonal and now that I've reached out I need some time to pull myself together."

"Just name the time and place and I'll be there."

"Friday night?"

"Text me your address and I'll pick you up."

"Seven o'clock?"

"See you then."

She disconnected and Steve faded from both of them, grateful for the relief he felt escaping the turmoil of his two sided emotional torment.

# CHAPTER THIRTY TWO

On Friday evening Steve followed Jon to an apartment building in Solana Beach. Jon paused at the front door and ran a comb through his hair and took a deep breath before knocking. Steve's heart dropped when a gaunt faced Heather answered, smiling weakly at Jon. She had dark circles under bloodshot eyes and her skin looked pale and sickly, but she looked beautiful in an ethereal way. Before Jon could say a word she broke down sobbing and he put his arms around her in awkward silence.

Steve's pain and helplessness surfaced like a reopened wound seasoned by the salt of jealousy from seeing her in Jon's arms. An urge to step in and try to inhabit Jon gripped him, but he remained steadfast.

"You all right?", Jon said, interrupting Steve's emotional chaos.

"I'm sorry." Heather stepped back and wiped tears from her eyes.

"It's all right." Jon pushed the hair back from her face. "There's no need to apologize. If you don't mind my saying, you look like shit but you're still as pretty as ever."

She laughed uneasily. "Thank you. I haven't been sleeping much. I have constant nightmares of Steve getting killed on his motorcycle over and over again."

Bastards, Steve thought.

"It's gotten so bad I'm afraid to go to sleep. I'm seeing a therapist, but..." She sobbed. "She gave me some Valium but it only made it worse."

Heather looked down and Jon took her chin in his hand and lifted her head up until their eyes met. "You're not the only one having nightmares. I was there when it happened and I've had more than my share. Mine don't seem to be as persistent, but I have an endless loop of that horrible night playing over and over in my head."

"I don't know what to do. I found your number on a note Steve left," Heather said. "I don't know why, but you were the only person I could think of to call. I didn't want to upset or burden Jaret and Amanda. She was so fond of him..."

"I'm glad you called."

She let out a long, shaky sigh.

He put his hand on her shoulder and stroked it. "Well now you're stuck with me whether you like it or not. What do you say we get a drink somewhere and talk things over."

Shit!, not alcohol, Steve thought.

"As long as I don't have to drive. I took a Valium before you came."

Jon held out his hand and bowed with a dramatic flourish. "Leave the driving to us."

Steve followed them to the Belly Up Tavern, a popular Solana Beach watering hole. It broke his heart to see Heather acting slow and mechanical with her aura at such a low ebb and beneath his sadness lurked a deep seated fear of what might happen.

They settled in to a corner booth and ordered Black Russians. After the waitress brought their drinks Jon held up his glass and tapped hers in a toast. "To Steve."

"That's really sweet of you to talk to me, Jon." Heather put her hand on his and Steve felt himself go rigid.

"I feel better with you here," she continued, speaking softly. "The pressure's been building and I had no way to let it out. My therapist doesn't seem to understand, but I feel like you do."

He patted her hand. "I've been going through the same things as you, only not quite as intense lately. Talking to you makes me feel better too."

"Really?"

"Sure."

They finished their drinks and made small talk, catching up on each other's lives, making Steve feel like the proverbial elephant in the room. His heart sank faster faster seeing how quickly Jon's aura dimmed with each sip while Heather's became barely visible.

"How about another drink?", Jon said draining his glass.

"As long as you're driving. I can feel the drink and Valium mixing, but it dulls the pain. Just to be safe I'd better have a wine cooler instead of more hard stuff."

He held up his hand, beckoning the waitress. "One last drink, then I'll get you home."

Jon ordered a beer for himself and a wine cooler, then excused himself to go to the men's room, leaving Heather alone. Her movements were clumsy and her eyes had a vacant look. When Jon came back Steve sensed a presence that he wished he didn't. It waxed stronger until a noticeable shift came over Heather. Jon didn't seem to notice, but to Steve it was unmistakable when he saw a thin vapor-like trail forming over her head. Her aura flickered and a subtle change came over her mannerisms. He saw it in the way she moved her hands and in her facial expressions, then a different look came to her eyes and in the next moment Steve peered into the dark seductive eyes of Carla looking right through him.

Fuck!

He felt so aware of her presence he feared she might sense him, but the more he studied her the more confident he became that she couldn't.

The waitress brought their drinks and Heather took a long sip.

"So tell me, Jon," she said. "Do you have any loves in your life?"

"Not right now. I've been having a hard time just keeping myself together."

She smiled and her eyes grew wide. "I haven't seen anybody since Steve."

"Maybe we can get together more often. Strictly as friends of course. What do you think?"

She licked her lips. "I'd like that."

"Great." Jon fidgeted with his napkin, then held up his beer. "Here's a toast to a renewed friendship."

She raised her glass.

"Cheers." He clinked his beer against her glass.

"These drinks are taking their toll," she said in a hushed tone. "I'm having a hell of a time keeping my equilibrium. What do you say we go back to my place before I make fools out of both of us."

"Sounds like a plan."

When they got up to leave, Steve felt hopeful when he noticed Carla struggling to control Heather's body.

A few minutes later Heather stumbled on the stairs to her apartment and nearly fell, but Jon caught her by the arm. "I'll get you safe inside, then I'd better get going."

She held him tighter. "Please don't go. Stay with me awhile longer. I feel so alone. Would you hold me awhile?"

Shit! Steve thought. Here we go.

They made their way to the couch where Jon put his arm around her looking stiff and uncomfortable. She responded by pressing herself hard against him and Steve sensed another unwelcome presence. Jon's aura fluttered and a thin wisp appeared over his head.

Steve put his attention on Jon and focused his energy on him. The intensity and frequency of the pulsations in his aura increased until it looked like a miniature, multicolored thunderstorm raged about Jon's head. The energies vacillated with increasing rapidity until Jon's aura appeared to shatter leaving nothing but low level energy and no red hue while Heather passed out. Jon sighed and closed his eyes, drifting off into his own slumber.

Steve relaxed and his mind flip-flopped until his anger dissipated and another part of him surfaced, willing to do anything to save Heather and Jon from the darkness, no matter the price. He sank into a morbid state of self-pity when a sweet soothing voice filled his mind.

*If I left you to face them alone, they'd have eaten you alive. You're not strong enough to withstand the two of them by yourself yet, but you're getting close.* He felt her gentle touch on his head. *I've been here with you the whole time, watching over you.*

Steve put his face in his hands. "I don't know if I can take this."

*If you keep thinking that way, you won't,* she said. *This is the time to be strong. I know this meeting has drained you emotionally, but there's no way around it if you're going to save them.*

"I know but..."

He looked up, not surprised to see that they were at Mick's spot. Teresa floated in front of him, her angelic presence suffused in a soft lavender radiance.

*My job is to support your positive side and insure that you become stronger through your experiences.*

"What made them decide to use Heather? She's got nothing to do with this."

*She was vulnerable and unwittingly left herself open for their manipulations which made her the perfect vehicle for making an attack on you and Jon. Carla's going to try and gain control of Jon through Heather the way she did with you. You know how jealous Carla is of her and how much she despises her. This approach is intended to satisfy her twisted sense of justice. The battle line is between Jon's lower and higher natures. If he can find it within himself to follow the guidance of his heart he'll save his soul and if he's strong enough he'll be instrumental in saving Heather's too. On the other hand, if he's weak he'll follow the seduction of the dark forces and they'll fall together.*

"Not if I can help it."

*Your task is to put aside your personal feelings and let go of everything no matter how much you love her, or how much it hurts. You can be a source of strength for them, but if you let your own desires get in the way you will contribute to their downfall.*

"I won't let that happen."

*If you can overcome the dark ones in this manner you'll be released from your earthly attachments.* She smiled beatifically. *You'll truly be a free spirit.*

With those words she faded from sight.

Steve went back and saw Heather wake up in Jon's arms. The gray light of dawn filtered in through her apartment windows. She looked up at Jon sleeping soundly and looked confused.

She slipped out of his arms, went to the closet and got a blanket. She studied him for a moment after covering him, then tiptoed to her bedroom, gently closing the door behind her.

Jon woke up a couple of hours later looking equally perplexed. He folded the blanket and quietly let himself out the front door, locking it behind him.

# CHAPTER THIRTY THREE

After watching a robust sparring class one night Steve joined Jon and Mick in Mick's kitchen to listen in on their conversation. Mick sat down at the kitchen table with two cans of La Croix water and handed one to Jon who popped the top and took a long sip while admiring the colorful visionary art work adorning Mick's walls.

"Pablo Amaringo," Mick said. "He was a famous Ayahuasca inspired visionary artist." Mick held up his can in a toast. "He was a friend of mine. He died a few years back. Those paintings are worth a few bucks now."

Jon held up his can and took another sip. "Steve said you were a shaman and that you went into the Amazon and worked with that Ayahuasca and other plants."

Mick held up a hand. "I'm no shaman and I don't call myself that. I'm just a curious person who has studied it all of my life. Among other things it's literally the world's oldest form of psychotherapy."

"I could sure use that. I've been trying to get my head together for awhile now, especially since Steve died, but I keep falling on my face. Spending time at the karate studio helps, but I know it's not the answer to all my problems."

Mick sipped his La Croix. "There's a lot to be said for discipline."

"I have to admit, I haven't been very disciplined. I've been drinking, smoking too much dope and snorting too much coke."

Mick looked him in the eye without any hint of judgment. "Steve was struggling with the same things and I have no doubt that it contributed to his end. I tried to reach out to him, but I think it was too little too late."

That was on me, Steve thought. You were there for me but I was too caught up in my own shit.

Jon stared at his can. "We were party buddies and he was partying at my house that night..."

"You helped him along," Mick said, "but you were just as lost as he was and from what you've been telling me you still are."

Jon looked up, eyes pleading. "Do you think drinking Ayahuasca can help? Can you get me some?"

Mick answered with a bemused smile. "First off, you'd have to clean up your act and knock off all that drinking and doping shit for awhile, then you'd have to prepare yourself for a night of puking and shitting where you might confront your darkest demons if you're lucky. It's not something I would get for you. It's taken in an all night ceremony led by a shaman."

"Puking and shitting?"

"In the jungle they call it *la purga*, the purge. It's not for everybody that's for sure. Aside from knocking off getting loaded all the time you have to follow a strict cleansing diet to prepare yourself and show the proper respect to the plant spirits."

*Bobinsana*, Steve thought. That's what Teresa was talking about.

John looked troubled. "Puking and shitting and facing demons too?"

"In the lore of the jungle all of that discomfort is the price you have to pay to prove that you are worthy of the gifts and wisdom that the plant spirits have to give you. If you think that is tough, try doing it with a bunch of other plants and mostly bland, tasteless food for ten days."

Jon's eyes grew wide. "That's what you did?"

"For about ten years now."

Jon shook his head. "Ten days of puking and shitting and eating tasteless food."

Mick smiled and held out his hands. "It's a growth process like a flower in bloom – and shit makes the best fertilizer." He chuckled. Do you think you're here to burn out on dope and alcohol?"

"No."

"You've been given the gift of life and a free will, so if you destroy yourself that's your choice."

Jon sat back and rubbed his chin. "That's wild. Do you think a person can reach perfection before they die?"

Mick shook his head. "That's the beauty of it. The unfolding process. The very fact that no one can become perfect makes the struggle meaningful. It's infinite!"

"You're serious, aren't you?"

"Serious as a heart attack." Mick hit the table with his palm. "To me the essence of life is to strive at every conceivable level. Don't get me wrong. I'm not against having fun along the way. Those things have their place, but as an end in themselves they're nothing but escapes from the miserable creatures we have made ourselves into."

"I have got to admit, things in my life have been pretty weird. I've been yearning for something. I keep thinking it's a woman. I know it's not dope, booze, or money, but when I'm around them I can't help myself."

"Been there, done that, lost the T-shirt."

Jon leaned forward and massaged his temples. "Now there's a lady who reappeared in my life." He looked up at Mick, meeting his penetrating eyes. "It's Steve's old girlfriend." He lowered his voice. "I have strong feelings for her and I think she needs me, but she has a strange effect on me."

His words rocked Steve.

Mick leaned forward and put his arms on the table. "What do you mean strange effect?"

"Part of me feels drawn to her but another part of me is deathly afraid. Whenever I'm around her my heart starts beating a mile a minute. No woman has ever affected me this way. I think I'm in love."

"Sounds more like lust to me. What are you afraid of?"

"She's got problems, but I think I can help."

"Before you consider helping anybody else you'd better make damn sure you've got your own act together."

"I don't really know her that well."

"All the more reason to be careful. I'm telling you, there are forces at work and they know your weak points."

Holy shit! Steve thought. He knows. Mick knows!

"Forces? What do you mean?"

"I don't think you realize it, but there are powerful forces working through us. In their hearts women long for a man they can turn to for strength but most of the men they find are weak and look to their women for strength and the women secretly resent them – and they have good reason to. It's not fair for them to shoulder the burden. More often than we care to admit both sexes are drawn to each other for the wrong reasons." He brought his hands together clasping them. "It really needs to be an equal and complementary partnership for it to succeed and neither one should need the other. They should be mutually independent."

"Sounds like I need to make some pretty drastic changes if I want to get my shit together," Jon said.

"You're better off taking things one step at a time."

Mick stood. "Listen Jon, I don't want to give you the bum's rush and I don't want to overload you with new ideas. When I get talking like this I could go for days," but I have to get up early for work tomorrow. If you want to talk some more let me know and I'll make more time. I have an amazing place I call my power spot up in the mountains near Julian where we can have a serious heart to heart."

"That sounds awesome. I'd like that!"

Mick held out his hand. "In all honesty I don't get to talk with many people about this kind of stuff. Think about what I've said and if you're still game we'll make it happen."

"I appreciate that!" Jon shook his hand. "I'll see you at the studio. Thanks for the talk."

# CHAPTER THIRTY FOUR

"Say-tan, Say-tan."

The chanting grew louder. Jon opened his eyes and found himself nude on an altar surrounded by his friends who all wore black hooded robes and took turns laughing and taunting him.

"You want perfection?" One said.

"Who do you think you are, Jesus Christ?" another chortled.

Someone threw beer and whiskey on him.

"You're a fucking fruitcake. Grab that bitch Heather and fuck her eyeballs out you pussy!"

Jon slid off the altar and bowed his head, wishing for help. When he looked up his tormentors had disappeared. Steve stood in their place with mountains and an expansive valley behind him. A softly glowing hummingbird hovered above them.

"Boy, am I glad to see you!" Jon said letting out a deep sigh.

"I'll bet you are," Steve answered.

"What a fucking bizarre dream. God, I'm so mixed up! I'm confused about Mick and I feel guilty about my feelings for Heather. I'll be betraying you by going out with her. I can't make heads or tails out of my feelings for her, and I can't wrap my head around Mick's ideas. He makes sense on one level, but puking and shitting my way to health?"

"Forget about my feelings for Heather. What's more important is her welfare. She's in trouble and you're the only one who can reach her." He looked down at himself and held his hands out. "Sure, I love her, but I have to put my feelings aside so we can save her. Other than meeting you here in your dreams there's nothing I can do in the physical world and aside from that I can't be sure that you'll remember any of this."

"What about Mick?" Jon looked down at himself fully clothed and his head jerked back in surprise. "It feels like Mick and Heather are pulling at me from different directions and I don't have the energy to go both ways."

Steve held up a hand. "Mick is the key to everything. Stop trying to make his ideas conform to what you think the truth is and open your perspective to accept his."

"How can Mick be the key? Why is he so important?"

"Before I checked out Mick tried to work with me the same way he's working with you only I didn't pay attention and like you I doubted him and because of that I was taken. If I'd listened to him, things would have turned out different. You're in the same predicament and you have the same choices I had. I lost my chance, but you still have yours."

Jon's expression scrunched up in confusion.

"Have faith in what feels right in your heart," Steve said. "You have to hang on to that with all your strength. It's the most potent weapon you have... "

A ringing sound made the hummingbird disappear and the surrounding mountains turn into a gray blur. Jon faded from the dream and Steve was yanked away, coming in focus to see Heather sitting up in bed drenched with sweat, clutching her cell phone. Her fluttering aura looked dull red and the glowing display of her digital clock said **2:00 AM**.

Jon's number rang without an answer. When she went disconnect his voice came on the line and once again Steve found himself in both places at the same time, fully aware of both as if they were the same place.

"Hello," Jon said groggily.

"Sorry for calling so late."

"What time is it?"

"After two."

"Is everything all right?"

"I'm okay, just scared. I couldn't sleep and needed someone to talk to."

"Give me a minute to wake up."

"I'm sorry. It was rude of me to call at this hour"

"Don't worry. I've been meaning to call you but I felt embarrassed after the other night."

"I felt the same way. I was afraid you'd get the wrong idea."

"Not at all. Truth be told I don't know what to think."

Heather opened her mouth to speak again, stopped, and swayed. Her aura dimmed.

"Heather?"

Her voice sounded husky and seductive. "Maybe we should try it again?"

After an uncomfortable silence Jon said, "Sure! I'd be glad to."

"I feel better already. We didn't really get to know each other very well last time. After we talked my nightmares went away but now they're back stronger than ever. That's what woke me tonight."

"I get it."

"Really?"

"We can talk about it when we get together."

"I... I..." Her voice shifted. "What did you just say?"

"We'll talk about it when we get together."

"Get together?"

"You sure you're all right?"

"I'm sorry. I lost my train of thought. You want to get together? That's fine. When?"

"Tomorrow night?"

"Sure," Heather said absentmindedly. "I feel like we got started on the wrong foot."

"Listen," Jon said in a low voice. "If you ever get scared in the middle of the night again don't hesitate to call. I don't care what time it is."

"Thank you Jon, that's sweet of you. I wouldn't bother you. It's just that I'm confused."

"Don't worry everything will work out."

"I feel better after talking to you. I think I can go back to sleep now. I'm going to let you go."

"See you tomorrow."

Heather hung up and took a deep breath, then laid back and closed her eyes, quickly falling asleep.

Steve snapped back to Jon who climbed out of bed and poured himself a shot of whiskey. He downed it and wiped his mouth with the back of his hand. After sitting immobile for awhile he went back to bed, but ended up staying awake most of the night.

# CHAPTER THIRTY FIVE

Steve sat with Jon and Heather at the Wild Note Cafe beside the Belly Up Tavern in Solana Beach feeling like an uneasy chaperone.

"That was a pretty strange time we had the other night," Jon said, draining the last of his vodka and tonic.

"Let's not talk about it." Heather stared down at her empty glass. "I'm kind of embarrassed."

"I'm sorry." He waved his hand as if brushing the thought away. "Forget it."

"Would either of you care for another drink?" The waiter said clearing dishes from their table.

"N – No – thank..." Heather's eyes went out of focus, her aura dimmed, and her voice deepened. "Thank you very much. I think I will."

Jon's eyes narrowed. "Okay. We'll have one more."

The waiter nodded and glanced sideways at Heather before leaving.

"What's the matter Jon?" She kicked off one of her shoes and caressed his leg with her foot.

"Whoa, Heather." He held his hands up. "Slow down."

She popped a Valium into her mouth and washed it down with the last of her wine.

"Damn, Heather." Jon shook his head. "What's wrong with you? You're eating those things like candy."

"Nothing, lover."

The waiter reappeared with their drinks.

"Bring me two shots of tequila please," Heather said.

The waiter looked at Heather and back to Jon who held up his hand and shook his head no.

Good man Jon, Steve thought.

"Don't give me that *No* shit." Heather's voice raised. "Give me the damn drinks." She pounded the table with her fist and the waiter stood frozen. She glared at him. "Move it, buster!"

He scurried away.

Jon took her by the hand. "What's gotten into you?"

She stared at him without answering.

The waiter came back and deposited the shots on the table and hurried away. Heather pushed one toward Jon and gulped the remaining one. "Drink it, then I'll tell you."

"But..."

"Don't but me, Jon. This is important. Drink it if you want to know what's going on."

Jon sighed and downed his shot, then hustled Heather out of the restaurant.

When they went through the door of her apartment, she "accidentally" fell into his arms, breathing hot in his ear. He pushed himself away, held her at arm's length, and guided her over to a chair. "I think you'd better have a seat."

"What the matter, Jon?" She giggled. "You afraid of me?"

"No! I just think we had too much to drink."

"You sure that's all it is or am I too much for you to handle?" She licked her lips sensuously.

"That's not it," Jon snapped.

"Then what are you talking about?" she said in an innocent tone.

"You know!"

"There's no need to get upset. I understand if you're not man enough to supply the needs of a woman like me." She ran her hands down the contours of her body. "Maybe you like guys instead?"

Jon didn't answer. His rage mounted by the second, evident in his blazing red aura. Heather went into the bedroom leaving him alone to sizzle.

He inhaled slow and deep to control himself, torn between following her into the bedroom and walking out the door.

"Come on in and join me if you're man enough to handle it," she taunted.

Jon stood immobile, unable to make a move either way. After a few indecisive minutes he burst into her room to find her passed out. He stared at her as his seething aura diminished and covered her with a blanket, then he let himself out the front door.

Shit's getting out of hand, Steve thought, but I have to give him credit. He held up and withstood the assault, only I don't know how long he'll be able to last.

With Heather unconscious and unaware Steve stayed with Jon watching over him as he drifted off to sleep. Barely audible voices filled his mind that he knew were directed at Jon.

*You might as well kill yourself. You can't win. Your life's not worth living.*

Steve tried to intervene and step into the conversation but he couldn't get through. All he could do was witness Jon slip deeper into a drunken slumber, and in this darkened dream state Jon went back to Heather's, drawn to her bedroom where he stood at her door for an interminable amount of time until the pressure became too much. He pushed open the door and stepped in.

A nude Heather draped herself across her bed beckoning for him to come to her side. He glided across the room as though pulled by a magnet through a thick carpet of mist and he laid down beside her, gazing deep into her eyes which looked like two shining embers.

Get out of there! Steve thought.

She put her arms around Jon and embraced him with a passionate kiss. A mild shock shook him when he tried to resist. The energy of it shook Steve to his core and an oppressive feeling of suffocation gripped him when he realized that he felt what Jon felt in this darkened state. The more he struggled the more trapped he felt.

Heather appeared to flow into him, paralyzing and permeating his whole being. An image of a preying mantis flickered in Steve's mind.

No! he screamed with every part of his being. Not again!

Heather disappeared and Jon materialized at Mick's power spot where Mick sat waiting. "I knew the two of you would come here." Mick looked from Steve to Jon and back again. "Those are some pretty tough odds you're up against."

"If it's any comfort," Steve said to Jon, "they damn near got me too."

"They?" Jon said. "That's no comfort."

Steve patted him hard on the back. "You keep getting shitfaced. That's an invitation."

"Heather's got me to the point where I don't know if I'm coming or going," Jon said. "She acts like two different people…"

"That's because she is," Steve said.

"What?"

"What Steve's trying to tell you," Mick said, "is that somebody else is working through Heather. That's whose got you confused, not Heather. They're trying to undermine you and by the looks of it they're doing a pretty good job."

"What can we do?"

"Quit playing their game by not getting fucked up all the time," Steve said. "Otherwise they're going to overcome you and Heather."

"If it wasn't for Heather I'd be doing fine."

Mick shook his head. "You can't blame her. You have to take responsibility for yourself."

"You have to confront her and see what happens," Steve continued. "It's dangerous, but a risk we have to take. There's no telling how our opponents will react, but if we wait much longer it will be too late. Heather is your weak point. That's what they're counting on. If you're firm the real Heather will sense your strength and be attracted to it."

Jon threw up his hands. "How will I know what to do? I'm not going to remember any of this when I wake up."

"You're right," Mick said, "but you'll have the pieces of the puzzle and you'll be inspired enough to look within for answers. It'll feel like you're on your own." He pointed back and forth between Steve and himself. "But we'll be guiding you and sending you energy in whatever ways we can."

"But that depends on how receptive you are to it and that depends on how fucked up you are," Steve added.

Before Jon could respond their surroundings faded, and Steve felt the energy pull him away to see Heather wake up in darkness, fully clothed and confused. She reached out and touched her nightstand lamp, then turned it on and squinted, looking around as if seeing her surroundings for the first time.

"What possessed me to get into bed fully clothed," she mumbled. "With a blanket? Was I sick?"

She laid immobile for a long time as a flurry of lost, puzzled expressions passed over her face.

"Shit!" She whispered, hitting herself with the palm of her hand. "I was out to dinner with Jon. Does he know I blacked out? He must have noticed. The only time I seem to black out is when I have anything to do with him. Is he responsible? If he is the cause he'll lie to me. If he's not he'll think I'm crazy."

She lay awake for a long time until tears flowed and she wept long into the night before drifting into a troubled sleep.

All Steve could do was watch.

# CHAPTER THIRTY SIX

Steve watched Jon stare at his bong on the table in front of him, clearly thinking about taking a hit. His mind whirled in a vortex of contradicting thoughts that he vocalized.

"I have to stay away from Heather."

"I have to help her."

"She wants me."

"I should go to bed with her."

"She needs help."

"She doesn't know what she's doing."

"She knows exactly what she's doing."

"I need a hit."

"No, it's trouble."

His aura fluctuated between dull red and pale blue so Steve focused on sending Jon positive thoughts and felt Jon drawing power from him when his aura pulsed blue and reflecting it back when it shone red. Jon's changing colors had a rhythm, so Steve timed his thoughts, increasing the energy when Jon pulsed blue and sending nothing when it turned red.

The changes came faster.

Steve kept up with them until Jon's aura looked like the flashing light from a police car, then he put everything he could into one last effort and the spinning red and blue flew off into the space around him and for a brief moment it looked as though he had no aura at all, then a pale blue emerged. It wasn't strong like Mick's, but blue nonetheless.

It's just a matter of time before it gets stronger, Steve thought. Carla and Elijah will have one hell of a time trying to influence him now.

Jon had his hand on his cell phone when it rang.

"Hello."

"Jon?"

"Heather! I was just thinking about calling you."

"I saved you the hassle. Stay where you are. I'll pick you up."

Jon looked shocked. "Sure. What have you got in mind?"

"I thought we might take a ride and enjoy the night."

"Okay. I have something I want to talk to you about anyway."

"I'll be right over."

Jon hit the End icon and looked lost. "Just one hit," he said, packing the bong. "I need to calm my nerves."

He heard the knock on his door a few minutes later. He answered and Heather strolled in and sat down on the arm of his couch. She had a twisted smile and a vacant look in her eyes. Her aura glimmered dull red.

Shit, Steve thought. Here it comes.

The more he studied her the more worried he became.

"You ready to go?" she said with a slur.

She's already half in the bag.

Jon grabbed his jacket. "Why don't I drive?"

"You always drive." She smirked. "Tonight you can leave the driving to us."

"You sure?"

"Don't be silly, Jon. You sound like an old lady. I got here in one piece, didn't I?"

Jon hesitated and she stared at him with her arms crossed.

He shrugged. "Okay, if that's the way you want it."

"That's the way I want it."

Once in Heather's Jetta, Steve saw a full moon rise above the horizon in a cloudless sky as they drove east on Highway Eight toward El Cajon in an uneasy silence that grew with each passing mile.

Something's going to happen, Steve thought. I know it.

"Heather," Jon said in an even tone. "We need to talk. I don't want to sound like a wet blanket, but all this business with the drinking and the pills has to stop."

She smiled at him and her sardonic look put Steve on edge more than any other time in the past.

"You're so right Jon." She jerked the steering wheel hard to the right, sending them careening off the road, smashing through a guard rail. Time passed in slow motion as it tumbled end over end down the embankment. The last thing Steve saw was a demented grimace frozen on Heather's face.

# CHAPTER THIRTY SEVEN

After a flash Steve watched Jon open his eyes blinking, lying on his back in grass. He sat up and peered into the darkness. A strange black form loomed close to where Jon sat. He stood and approached it, stopping when he got within a few yards of it.

A wave of shock passed through Steve when he saw Heather's overturned Jetta. He moved closer and Jon lunged toward the car, panicking. Inside it Steve saw the dark forms of two limp bodies.

Jon reached for the door and his fingers went through it. He drew back his hand and examined it, shocked to see it translucent. He stumbled around to the front of the car and recognized the lifeless body of Heather behind the steering wheel.

"This can't be. Oh my God, I'm dead! Heather!" he screamed.

She didn't answer.

He sobbed with his head in his hands until Heather's voice shocked him. "Jon?"

His mouth dropped open.

Confusion overwhelmed Steve when the shadowy forms of Carla and Elijah came up the hill and terror filled him when he understood what was happening. Knowing that they couldn't see him and were unaware of his presence had the effect of amplifying his fear for Jon.

"It's all right Jon," Elijah said, mimicking Steve's voice. "We're together now."

Jon's eyes widened. "Steve! Heather!" He whispered. "Where did you? How? What's happening?"

"He's right, Jon," Carla added in Heather's voice. "Come with us. We have a lot to show you."

Jon clenched his fists and pulled at his hair. "It's not fair," he screamed. His voice faded into the darkness. He opened his mouth to scream again, stopped and buried his face in his hands again. "It's not fair," he mumbled.

Steve wanted to scream himself, but no one would hear.

"Come on, honey," Carla said in Heather's voice. She extended her hand.

Jon walked toward them, then stopped and turned back toward the car.

"Don't look back!" Elijah ordered.

"There's no need to look," Carla said in a soothing tone. "It'll only cause you more unhappiness. This doesn't have to be a painful experience. Come with us. We'll take care of you."

Jon looked from Elijah to Carla and back again. She smiled at him and winked.

"Something's not right", he said.

"There's no need to be afraid," Elijah said. "She's had a little problem with her pills, that's all. You can't hold that against her." He wagged a finger. "You haven't exactly been an angel yourself. Don't worry. You can trust me."

Jon took a few more steps toward them and something from the Jetta yanked him to the ground.

"It's okay Jon," Elijah reassured him. "That's just your old attachment to your physical body."

Jon looked down at his midsection and saw a tiny silver cord attached to some inner part of him. He turned back toward the car. Now that it had pulled tight it became visible.

"Don't worry, Jon," Carla said. "We'll help you."

Before he could respond Elijah and Carla got on each side of him and pulled him along with them making his gossamer cord glisten with a sparkling light of it's own. It stretched like a rubber band, but held fast without breaking.

"You have to help us," Elijah said with urgency. "Let go with your mind. Let go with your heart. It's time."

Elijah and Carla pulled harder, stretching Jon's cord almost to the breaking point. Sparks flew. While they pulled Steve saw their combined energies flowing into Jon, undermining his resistance.

"Let go with your mind," Elijah repeated.

"Let go with your heart," Carla added. "Don't fight. Come with us," she continued in a soft breathy voice. "We love you," she half-whispered.

Jon pulled back. "God help me."

Please, Steve thought, both calling in and sending every bit of energy he could conceptualize. Help us Teresa!

A bright shimmering violet electric current came racing up Jon's cord and a powerful calming presence flew into Steve's core, extending out to Jon. Different sets of instantaneous thoughts filled Steve and he knew that he and Jon shared the experience. Each jolt destroyed the one preceding it.

*There is no God.*

\*God exists. Love.\*

*Hate.*

\*Life.\*

*Death.*

\*Growth.\*

*Decay*

\*Light.\*

*Darkness.*

I have to choose.

*There's no choice, no hope.*

Darkness swallowed them, held back by an incandescent lavender glimmer.

\*Go to the light.\*

*Darkness Rules. There is no light.*

It faded.

Yes, yes, there is.

It brightened.

There is light.

"I want the light," Jon said. "More than anything I want to follow my heart. I don't want to be dominated against my will. I can choose between light and darkness and I. Want. The. Light!"

Jon and Steve illuminated with the force of the growing ultraviolet light that had entered through Jon's cord and the two invading energies retreated back into Elijah and Carla. The light pursued them flowing through Steve to Jon and into them.

The simultaneous shrieking of Carla and Elijah pierced every fiber of his being and their eyes became two sets of blazing embers. Their bodies shimmered brighter as their features contorted into a pair of distorted reptilian looking creatures, then one unified tormented scream filled the night as their misshapen bodies radiated a blinding ultraviolet light that exploded in a spectacular incandescent shower. Jon's light filled body streaked back toward the car in a lavender flash and everything went black.

# CHAPTER THIRTY EIGHT

Steve popped into Mick's power spot with a serenity he had never known before combined with a sense of belonging.

"I must be dead," Jon said rubbing his palm on his chest. "It's not as bad as I thought."

*I hate to disappoint you partner,* Steve's said, *but you couldn't be any more alive.*

Jon looked at Steve, incredulous. Steve nodded, delighted that his mouth didn't move and his voice seemed to come from everywhere.

"What the hell's going on?"

*This is more like a dream,* Steve continued.

Jon frowned. "What's happening?"

*You could say we've graduated,* Steve answered.

Teresa appeared, suffused in a warm lavender radiance that Steve both saw and felt. *Better let me explain,* she said.

Jon looked at her, enraptured.

She blessed him with a loving gaze. *How are you doing, brother?*

Though she spoke to Jon her directionless voice echoed inside Steve's head.

"Fine," Jon answered. "Only I wish somebody would tell me what's going on. I'm losing my marbles."

*You and Steve have raised in consciousness and developed a special relationship with each other. One that's identical to the one Steve and I have."

"What kind of a relationship?"

The words came to Steve effortlessly. *Teresa is what you'd call my guardian angel, and I'm now yours. She works with me by inspiring me. She can only do this because I've aligned myself with her. Any good I've ever done with you came through me by her guiding me through my intuition. The relationship I have with you on the material plane is a kind of holographic duplicate of the one she has with me filtered down from higher realms. I'm fully aware of this and I have total freedom, but my will and motivation are no different from hers.*

"And we have the same relationship?"

"That's right."

"Why don't you talk normally any more?"

Teresa's smile grew, lighting up their surroundings. *He doesn't need to. He's raised his consciousness to the point where he can communicate telepathically.*

"Was it you guys who bailed me out?" Jon paused. "I think I understand. They were forcing their wills on me."

*They knew they had you off balance," Steve said, *and they might have gotten to you, but your heart was in the right place.*

Jon fell silent and looked distracted. Steve felt it along with him and the thought struck him in the same moment Jon blurted, "Heather!"

In the next instant Steve stood by Jon's hospital bed where Jon woke up frantically calling, "Heather!" He screamed it three or four times before a nurse came rushing in.

"Calm down," she said. "You're all right. A little banged up, but there's no serious damage."

"It's not me I'm worried about, it's Heather."

"I'm sorry... "

"No..." he cried. "Please, God, no!"

"At least you made it," the nurse said in an awkward effort to console him. "I'm sorry."

Steve felt numb from the loss. I never thought we'd lose Heather, he thought, feeling abandoned. I can't understand where we went wrong.

In the next moment he stood beside her, forcing himself to take a final look at her lifeless body lying on the hospital gurney where she appeared to be resting peacefully.

I'm responsible for her death, he thought. Because of me they have her. I can't believe Teresa would let the dark ones take her so easily.

When the doctor moved in to cover her head it was more than Steve could bear. The act of pulling the sheet up was the final proof that she had gone. Steve struggled to fight back his emotion.

He turned to leave before the doctor finished and found himself facing Teresa's tender, loving gaze. He looked into her eyes searching for an answer. *Why, Teresa? Why? Why do you of all people want to prolong my suffering?*

She motioned for him to turn back toward Heather. He hesitated, then turned to see Heather's aura "pop" on like the blue flame on a gas pilot and she opened her eyes.

"Where am I?" she asked, looking up into the shocked face of the doctor.

# AUTHOR'S NOTE

When I was a senior in high school I had a close friend, an only child who came home to find his mother's three day old stinking blue corpse suffocated with a plastic bag over her head from an apparent suicide. His grisly discovery at the age of eighteen changed him and had repercussions that profoundly influenced my life's path.

Soon after her passing we were out drinking with friends. He understandably drank to excess and became another person from the one we had known when he flew into an antagonistic rage, attacking everyone within striking range. We tried to control him, but he acted like he didn't know us and became the classic example of "the lights are on, but nobody's home", and his violence knew no bounds. One of my buddies thought we should knock him out, so someone held him and the one with the idea punched him in the face a number of times breaking his cheek and jaw, but he would not go out. He only raged harder. I couldn't watch anymore, so I intervened and spent hours wrestling and restraining him in the back seat of a car slipping and sliding around in a puddle of puke, piss, and blood.

Throughout this disturbing incident one of his eyes looked off to one side with a disconnected demonic gleam that seemed to be fixed on some other place that we were not a part of, and whatever intelligence or lack of intelligence that was behind that eye, it was not our friend. It was most decidedly otherworldly creepy.

I finally managed to get him home and into bed where he eventually settled down and passed out, waking the next morning beaten, bruised, broken, and caked with blood and no memory of anything that had happened. It hurt to even look at him.

That demonic otherworldly look haunted me and marked my fascination with possession, demonic and otherwise, and this fascination was fueled in that same time frame when my mother came to me early one night, looked me in the eye and handed me *The Exorcist* by William Peter Blatty, saying, "You have to read this."

I went into my bedroom and started reading it at seven-thirty on a school night and came out of my bedroom at seven thirty in the morning after finishing it. I could not put that book down. The movie soon followed and became a cultural phenomena, cementing my already riveted fascination.

As a result of those experiences it dawned on me that alcohol was referred to as *spirits* and after the horror I had experienced with my disturbed friend, in my mind the connection was all too real.

I came to my conclusions about alcohol and spirits many years before the internet existed and had never seen any references to what I had come to believe through my experiences, so thirty six years after my first attempt at writing a novel I resurrected it and between drafts I looked it up on the internet. To my amazement I discovered the following recently written reference on a web site called Auricmedia.

**The word "alcohol" is said to come from the arabic term "Al-khul" which means "BODY-EATING SPIRIT" and the origin of the term "ghoul", but this** etymology of 'alcohol' is untrue. This definition, 'Al-kuhl, flesh eating demon' was given in a 2016 science fiction/horror thriller film called The Dark Tapes, but it has not been corroborated by any dictionaries or etymological listings. Nonetheless these beliefs persist.

**In alchemy, alcohol is used to extract the soul essence of an entity. Hence its' use in extracting essences for essential oils, and the sterilization of medical instruments. By consuming alcohol into the body, it in effect extracts the very essence of the soul, allowing the body to be more susceptible to neighboring entities most of which are of low frequencies. (why do you think we call certain alcoholic beverages "SPIRITS"). That is why people who consume excessive amounts of alcohol often black out, not remembering what happened. This happens when the good soul**

(we were sent here with) leaves because the living conditions are too polluted and too traumatic to tolerate. The good soul jettisons the body, staying connected on a tether, and a dark entity takes the body for a joy ride around the block, often in a hedonistic and self serving illogical rampage. Our bodies are cars for spirits. If one leaves, another can take the car for a ride.

Essentially when someone goes dark after drinking alcohol or polluting themselves in many other ways, their body often becomes possessed by another entity. Have you ever felt different, more sexual, more violent, less rational and less logical.........after drinking alcohol? Are you aware we already live inside an ancient religious cult who are schooled concerning the dark powers of alcohol? It is this cult that popularizes alcohol, through the media and government it controls, to serve a very ancient and dark agenda.

The solutions to our crumbling society are only to be found within our non polluted collective humanity, not within modern science and the death cult it represents, Our dark and immoral human farmers masquerade as altruistic governments, who then serve us up to dark spiritual entities that feed off our energies when we consume alcohol and a host of other toxic substances they rain down from the top of the ruling pyramid. We're slaves living on an elaborate control grid.....based on indoctrination, propaganda, chemical sedation, toxic medication and we're even used as food energy for dark spirits who live outside the frequency of visible sight. I haven't drank alcohol in almost 5 years. Now, the dark spirits are in fear of me and that's the way it was always meant to be. Join the moral rebirth of humanity, unslave, reject the poison and lets get to work doing what we know has to be done.

http://www.auricmedia.net/alcohol-said-come-arabic-term-al-khul-means-body-eating-spirit

Early in the nineteen-eighties I was studying martial arts and riding my motorcycle in San Diego when a recently divorced guy named Steve who was also from Boston came to study at the studio. We became instant friends, studying karate together and riding our motorcycles throughout Southern California until that tragic day a few short months later when I tried to reach him and discovered that he had been killed on his motorcycle.

Growing up in the Boston neighborhood of Dorchester I had many friends who died from drownings, shootings, stabbings, electrocution, suicides, and accidents, not to mention getting their heads blown off in a back alley, framed and murdered by the cops, so I was no stranger to death, but something about my buddy Steve getting cut down at that point in his life with so much promise sent me into a depression that I could not shake, so I started writing.

*AfterLife* was my first novel, written close to forty years ago in an effort to process Steve's death. I spent five years on those early drafts, writing it out longhand on legal pads in pencil, giving myself carpal tunnel syndrome for my efforts, and a few more years in writing workshops trying to make it worthy of publication, but being my first novel, it never found publication, so I shelved it and moved on.

Fast forward to present day with thirty years of teaching dramatic writing under my belt, seventeen writing awards, thirteen books in print, numerous short stories, a play, screenplays, and a producing and directing credit, and through the magic of an amazing open source program called **LibreOffice** I was able to import the original **Wordstar** 1.0 file into its word processor and with a bit of massaging resurrected that first attempt at a novel and through extensive rewriting was able to mentor my thirty year old self.

*AfterLife* is my fourteenth published book.

Alcohol has nearly destroyed my life and in one of life's ironies the destruction that it brought me came from other people's drinking, not my own. Needless to say I have no use for it and see it as a seductive agent that ultimately diminishes awareness, bringing with it death, disease, and destruction.

Psychedelics?

They are another story entirely.

Suffice it to say, ***Spirit Matters***.

# ABOUT THE AUTHOR

Matthew J. Pallamary's works have been translated into Spanish, Portuguese, Italian, Norwegian, French, and German. His historical novel of first contact between shamans and Jesuits in 18th century South America, titled, *Land Without Evil* received rave reviews along with a San Diego Book Award for mainstream fiction. It was also adapted into a full-length stage and sky show, co-written with Agent Red, directed by Agent Red, and performed by Sky Candy, an Austin Texas aerial group. The making of the show was the subject of a PBS series, Arts in Context episode, which garnered an EMMY nomination.

His nonfiction book, *The Infinity Zone: A Transcendent Approach to Peak Performance* is a collaboration with professional tennis coach Paul Mayberry that offers a fascinating exploration of the phenomenon that occurs at the nexus of perfect form and motion. *The Infinity Zone* took 1ˢᵗ place in the International Book Awards, New Age category and was a finalist in the San Diego Book Awards.

His first book, a short story collection titled *The Small Dark Room of the Soul* was mentioned in The Year's Best Horror and Fantasy and received praise from Ray Bradbury. *The Small Dark Room of the Soul* is also available as an audio book.

His second collection, *A Short Walk to the Other Side* was an Award Winning Finalist in the International Book Awards, an Award Winning Finalist in the USA Best Book Awards, and an Award Winning Finalist in the San Diego Book Awards. *A Short Walk to the Other Side* is also available as an audio book.

*DreamLand* a novel about computer generated dreaming, written with legendary DJ Ken Reeth won first place in the Independent e-Book Award in the Horror/Thriller category and was an Award Winning Finalist in the San Diego Book Awards.

It's sequel, *n0thing* is titled after the main character, who in the real world is his nephew, an international Counter-Strike gaming champion. After winning what amounts to the Super Bowl of gaming, n0thing and his winning teammates, are recruited as a literal "dream team" whose mission is to go into the nightmares of battle scarred veterans and rescue them from their traumatic memories while becoming ambassadors for a gaming platform that exceeds virtual reality with an experience that pushes the boundaries of reality itself.

*Eye of the Predator* was an Award Winning Finalist in the Visionary Fiction category of the International Book Awards. *Eye of the Predator* is a supernatural thriller about a zoologist who discovers that he can go into the minds of animals.

*CyberChrist* was an Award Winning Finalist in the Thriller/Adventure category of the International Book Awards. *CyberChrist* is the story of a prize winning journalist who receives an email from a man who claims to have discovered immortality by turning off the aging gene in a 15 year old boy with an aging disorder. The forwarded email becomes the basis for an online church built around the boy, calling him CyberChrist.

***Phantastic Fiction - A Shamanic Approach to Story*** took first place in the International Book Awards Writing/Publishing category. ***Phantastic Fiction*** is Matt's guide to dramatic writing that grew out of his popular Phantastic Fiction Workshop.

***Night Whispers*** was an Award Winning Finalist in the Horror category of the International Book Awards. Set in the Boston neighborhood of Dorchester, ***Night Whispers*** is the story of Nick Powers, who loses consciousness after crashing in a stolen car and comes to hearing whispering voices in his mind. When he sees a homeless man arguing with himself, Nick realizes that the whispers in his head are the other side of the argument. ***Night Whispers*** is also available as an audio book.

His memoir ***Spirit Matters*** detailing his journeys to Peru, working with shamanic plant medicines took first place in the San Diego Book Awards Spiritual Book Category, and was an Award-Winning Finalist in the autobiography/memoir category of the National Best Book Awards. ***Spirit Matters*** is also available as an audio book.

Matt has also produced and directed ***The Santa Barbara Writers Conference Scrapbook*** documentary film and co-wrote the book of the same title in collaboration with Y. Armando Nieto, and conference founder Mary Conrad.

***The Center Of The Universe Is Right Between Your Eyes But Home Is Where The Heart Is*** was an Award Winning Finalist in the International Book Awards. Based on a lifetime of research into shamanism, visionary states, the evolution of written communication and the roots of storytelling, award-winning author, editor, and shamanic explorer Matthew J. Pallamary takes those with open minds courageous enough to question the illusions that most of us think of as real on an expansive journey that pierces the veil of reality itself.

His work has appeared in Oui, New Dimensions, The Iconoclast, Starbright, Infinity, Passport, The Short Story Digest, Redcat, The San Diego Writer's Monthly, Connotations, Phantasm, Essentially You, The Haven Journal, The Montecito Journal, and many others. His fiction has been featured in The San Diego Union Tribune which he has also reviewed books for, and his work has been heard on KPBS-FM in San Diego, KUCI FM in Irvine, television Channel Three in Santa Barbara, and The Susan Cameron Block Show in Vancouver. He has been a guest on the following nationally syndicated talk shows; Paul Rodriguez, In The Light with Michelle Whitedove, Susun Weed, Medicine Woman, Inner Journey with Greg Friedman, and Environmental Directions Radio series. Matt has appeared on the following television shows; Bridging Heaven and Earth, Elyssa's Raw and Wild Food Show, Things That Matter, Literary Gumbo, Indie Authors TV, and ECONEWS. He has also been a frequent guest on numerous podcasts, among them, The Psychedelic Salon, Black Light in the Attic, Third Eye Drops, C-Realm, Psychedelics Today, Voices in the Dark, Adventures Through the Mind, Beyond the Veil, and others.

Matt received the Man of the Year Award from San Diego Writer's Monthly Magazine and has taught a fiction workshop at the **Southern California Writers' Conference** in San Diego, Palm Springs, and Los Angeles, and at the **Santa Barbara Writers' Conference** for thirty years. He has lectured at the Greater Los Angeles Writer's Conference, the Getting It Write conference in Oregon, the Saddleback Writers' Conference, the Rio Grande Writers' Seminar, the National Council of Teachers of English, The San Diego Writer's and Editor's Guild, The San Diego Book Publicists, The Pacific Institute for Professional Writing, The 805 Writers Conference, and he has been a panelist at the World Fantasy Convention, Con-Dor, and Coppercon. He is presently Editor in Chief of Mystic Ink Publishing.

Matt was a featured lecturer and performer at the **Mysteries of the Amazon** exhibit at the Appleton Museum in Ocala Florida and frequently visits the mountains, deserts, and jungles of North, Central, and South America pursuing his studies of shamanism.

**WWW.MATTPALLAMARY.COM**

# BOOKS BY MATTHEW J. PALLAMARY

THE SMALL DARK ROOM OF THE SOUL

LAND WITHOUT EVIL

SPIRIT MATTERS

DREAMLAND (WITH KEN REETH)

THE INFINITY ZONE (WITH PAUL MAYBERRY)

A SHORT WALK TO THE OTHER SIDE

CYBERCHRIST

EYE OF THE PREDATOR

PHANTASTIC FICTION

NIGHT WHISPERS

N0THING

THE SANTA BARABARA WRITERS CONFERENCE SCRAPBOOK
(WITH MARY CONRAD & Y. ARMANDO NIETO)

THE CENTER OF THE UNIVERSE
IS RIGHT BETWEEN YOUR EYES
BUT HOME IS WHERE THE HEART IS

www.ingramcontent.com/pod-product-compliance
Lightning Source LLC
Chambersburg PA
CBHW070113260626
47160CB00004B/1454